Net Gain

Helen Parker

By the same author:
Let the Land Breathe

Cover design: Paul Airy
Cover illustration: Colin Smithson

Scripture Union, 207–209 Queensway, Bletchley, Milton Keynes, MK2 2EB, England.
Email: info@scriptureunion.org.uk
Website: www.scriptureunion.org.uk

ISBN 1 85999 632 9

British Library Cataloguing-in-Publication Data.
A catalogue record of this book is available from the British Library.

Printed and bound in Great Britain by Creative Print and Design (Wales) Ebbw Vale.

Scripture Union is an international Christian charity working with churches in more than 130 countries, providing resources to bring the good news about Jesus Christ to children, young people and families and to encourage them to develop spiritually through the Bible and prayer.

As well as our network of volunteers, staff and associates who run holidays, church-based events and school Christian groups, we produce a wide range of publications and support those who use our resources through training programmes.

Contents

For Dara and Ross

Chapter 1

The old lifeboat station

"Come on, slowcoach, I'll beat you to the top!"
Steven called over his shoulder.

"No chance!" Graeme puffed, trying to catch up.

Steven grinned confidently. Even though he was
shorter than Graeme, he knew he would beat him.
He could always run faster, climb higher or ride his
bicycle harder than any of his friends.

As always, Steven arrived first, and leaned his
elbows on the natural log fence which he and his
dad had built around the top ground. Graeme
followed, panting, and together they stared out
over the caravans and Farmer MacKay's fields to
the coast. From this position on Hooper's Reach,
the highest point of land, they could just see the sea,
a narrow ribbon of blue, shimmering in the April
sunshine.

"I found out about the legend," Steven
commented. "About Hooper."

"Who was he?"

"He was an Irish sailor. He used to sail to this
part of the west coast of Scotland to visit his
girlfriend. She used to light two fires, one on this
high point, like a beacon, and one lower down.
When the fires lined up in his sights, Hooper knew
he could sail his craft safely between the rocks."

Turning round to lean his back against the fence,

Steven looked inland, at the star-shaped grassy area in front of him and the Scots pine trees beyond. Graeme turned as well.

"It would be criminal to put caravans up here," Graeme reflected. "You were right, Steve, when you said we should let the land breathe. Think of the wildlife habitats which would be destroyed if Hooper's Reach was dug up."

"Dad keeps reminding me that anyone on the caravan site is allowed to come up here, but I still feel it's ours. Our special place. It's always belonged to Lucy and me. Er, and you, of course."

"I haven't been up here since we played tricks on Alexander Curtis," Graeme observed.

"Don't remind me," Steven groaned. "I got into terrible trouble for that."

"Still no news of the Curtis family, then?" Graeme asked.

"None at all. As soon as the lawyers got involved, and stopped Mr Curtis' plans to dig up Hooper's Reach, they moved suddenly. Disappeared overnight. Didn't say where they were going."

"Well, good riddance to them! I'm glad they've gone!"

"I think Alexander was OK really. So was his mum. It was just his dad..."

"Is the hide still there?" Graeme interrupted, peering among the trees.

"Yeah. It's well camouflaged from here. Come and look." They crossed the grassy area and made their way between the trees to the place where Steven had rigged up an old green tent, with a slit at eye-level where he could watch birds without being seen. The two of them stood, motionless for a minute or two, but Steven wasn't in the mood for stillness. "I'm thirsty," he said. "Let's go to my house for a drink."

They jogged down the hill between the caravans to the warden's cottage at the bottom of the site and burst in at the back door. Steven's dad was just leaving.

"Hi son. Hello, Graeme. I'm just going to mend a leaking tap in one of the top caravans, and Mum and Lucy are going to Reception in a minute, so make sure you take your key if you go out. OK?"

"OK, Dad. We just came back for a drink."

The phone rang, and Steven's dad went into the hall to answer it. Steven reached two glasses from the cupboard, and took a carton of juice from the fridge.

"That's all settled then!" Steven's dad announced, reappearing from the hall.

"What is?" Steven and Graeme asked together.

"Sandy Campbell's coming with us on the Holiday Club Quiz Walk."

"Who?" Steven and Graeme asked.

"The what?" Mum and Lucy asked, appearing in the kitchen.

"The Holiday Club Quiz Walk, Mum!" Steven told her. "It's just for the older kids from the Holiday Club. We're going to take the cliff path up to Westerley Point, then have a picnic on the beach..."

"...And it's a quiz!" Lucy added, "With rhyming clues. And there's a prize for the winner!"

"Dad, who's Sandy Campbell?" Steven asked again.

"He's a policeman. His wife was brought up in

the village and he's on the village council. Sandy's been working and living in the Old Town for quite a while, but he and his wife have just moved into the village. When he heard about the Holiday Club, he said he'd be happy to help."

About twelve kids and three adults assembled outside the village hall on the morning of the Quiz Walk.

Steven's dad introduced Sandy Campbell to the children. "These two are mine," he announced, with one hand on Steven's shoulder and the other on Lucy's.

"Hi kids!" Sandy grinned, looking from one to the other. "I can tell you're a MacGregor, Steven. You've got your dad's hair and eyes, but as for this redhead..." He looked at Lucy.

"She looks like Mum," Steven explained. "Dad calls them his fiery females!"

"And this blonde cover girl is Amanda!" Steven's dad went on. Amanda blushed at the compliment, but Steven silently agreed that Amanda was pretty enough for the front cover of a magazine. "She lives in the village now," Steven's dad continued, "and she's going to start at the high school this autumn, along with our Steven and several of the others..."

"And this is Graeme Robertson," Steven interrupted, standing beside his friend. "He lives in Manchester, but his family has a caravan on the site, and they always come for holidays."

"Pleased to meet you," Graeme said, shaking Sandy Campbell's hand solemnly.

When the introductions were finished, Mr Campbell promised to try to remember everyone's name, and they set off at a brisk pace, chattering and filling in their quiz sheets as they went. They slowed down once they reached the steep cliff path and everyone fell silent because they needed all their breath for the uphill climb. They felt exhilarated when they reached the top.

"Wow! We're on the roof of the world!" Steven exclaimed, reaching up as if he could touch the sky.

Graeme arrived to join him. "How high are we, Mr MacGregor?" he asked, turning to Steven's dad, and gasping with the effort of the climb.

"I don't know precisely, but they say..."

"...It's the highest point between here and America," Steven and Lucy chorused, knowing exactly what their dad would say. The three of them laughed and Graeme joined in.

"It feels like it!" he agreed. "I haven't been up here since last summer. I'd forgotten how high it was!"

"I expect this bit used to be part of the Great Caledonian Pine Forest," said Lucy importantly. The other children joined them, some of them peeling off jackets or jumpers despite the April breeze. Mrs MacKenzie, the minister's wife, arrived finally, her cheerful, round face red with effort.

"What's this clue? I'm stuck on number 5," said Amanda, waving her clipboard and quiz sheet. "Fossil fuel found on the top of the hill. Rhymes with 'feet'," she read.

"Easy!" said Lucy. "Peat!"

"This isn't fuel, it's a trampoline!" Mr Campbell declared, bounding in big circles around the panting, chattering group. "Look at me! Moonwalking!"

"Bet you wish you could run like that when you're catching criminals, Mr Campbell," Steven grinned.

"You're right there, Steven. Mind you, I don't do many dramatic runs. It's not quite like on TV, you know!"

"What's hemlock, Dad?" Lucy asked, puzzling over her quiz sheet.

"It's a poisonous plant."

"Does it grow here?" she frowned, gazing around.

"No. Look, it's something that rhymes with hemlock," Graeme pointed out. "Unpolished jewel."

"Whatever is it?" Lucy scratched her head, puzzled. The other girls gathered round her, but no one could work it out.

"No idea," Graeme admitted, and Steven agreed.

"I've got it!" Amanda announced suddenly. "Gem rock! Of course! There are lots of semi-precious gemstones in the hills and cliffs. There are garnets and agates... they're lovely, a sort of turquoise." The others were staring at her, open-mouthed. She laughed. "My aunty Carrie's got a tumble polisher. She makes semi-precious gemstones into jewellery," she explained. "I bet we can find some on the beach. There might..."

"Look everyone!" Mrs MacKenzie burst out, "Seals!"

The children stood still and peered out to sea. Steven's dad fished out his binoculars and passed them round, so that everyone could watch the two seals frolicking in the distance amongst the rocks offshore.

10

"They're playing 'tag'!" Mr Campbell said. "No, follow-the-leader! No, hide-and-seek!"

"Sandy Campbell, you're just a big kid!" Mrs MacKenzie teased him. He grinned, and Steven thought he was well named, with his sandy-coloured hair and freckled face.

"Let's stop for a drink and catch our breath, everyone, then we'll take the cliff path down to the beach and the old Westerley Point lifeboat station," Steven's dad said. He slipped his rucksack off his back and got out a large bottle of squash and a dozen plastic cups. He poured juice and Mrs MacKenzie passed it round. Graeme looked for a comfortable tuft for a seat.

"Don't sit down, Graeme," Mrs MacKenzie said suddenly. "The peat's soft and springy, but it's water-logged. You'll have a wet backside."

"But I thought Scottish people used to use peat for fuel on their cottage fires in the crofts," Graeme said.

"They still do, especially in the Hebrides," Steven's dad assured him. "They cut it out of the hillside in neat brick-shaped chunks and stack it up to drain and dry. Then it burns very hot once it's thoroughly alight."

"Wow! Free heating! Must tell my gran!" Graeme grinned.

"But peat's a fossil fuel," Steven argued. "It'll run out in the end, like coal and electricity."

"That's why we use low-energy light bulbs and stuff like that on the caravan site," Lucy added proudly.

"Come on, everyone. Let's go down and see if we can find any gem rocks," said Mr Campbell, leading a slow, steady procession down the steep, stony cliff path, and chatting enthusiastically with the children. Everyone followed, leaving Steven's dad to bring up the rear.

At the bottom of the cliff, everyone poked around in rock pools and filled in more of their quiz sheets until Mrs MacKenzie found a good, dry, rocky area where they could sit and eat their packed lunches. She fussed and clucked around them all like a mother hen. Then she checked that they hadn't left any litter before they all walked along the beach to the old lifeboat station.

"Look, Dad, all the windows are broken," Steven said. "It wasn't that bad last year."

"What a pity," his dad replied. "Seems a shame to let the old place become desolate."

"It hasn't been in use for a couple of years now," Mr Campbell explained. "What the weather didn't do, the vandals have finished off."

"They must have been energetic vandals! It's so far!" Amanda objected, looking back up the cliff path.

"Not by road," said Mr Campbell, pointing. "We came by the scenic route! But remember it's really only a few minutes from the village by car or bus."

"What happens if someone's boat capsizes, or a swimmer drifts out to sea?" Lucy asked.

"Someone alerts SAR – Search and Rescue," Mr Campbell explained, "and they send out a Sea King helicopter from HMS Gannet, the Royal Naval Aid Station at Prestwick..."

"And they winch someone up from the sea into the helicopter?" Graeme asked eagerly.

"Wow! A helicopter ride! I'd love to do that!" Steven interrupted.

"Don't get the idea that it's fun," Mr Campbell warned them, unusually serious for a moment. "These coasts can be treacherous, even for people who know the sea. But the helicopter can get a better view than the old lifeboat could."

The children jostled to get a better look inside. Steven was surprised to find the building was in quite good condition apart from the windows. There were two big rooms at the front, kitchen and toilets at the back, and the boathouse with the slipway right outside. He imagined being a lifeboat man on a stormy night with wind, rain and waves howling and lashing all around. Then he tried to imagine the beach and the cliffs on a still, clear winter's day, with gulls and gannets wheeling round, and waders scavenging among the rock pools. He'd seen videos of the local wildlife at the visitors' centre at the Deer Park, where he and Lucy had been with Graeme's family, and suddenly he had a brainwave.

"This building ought to be a visitors' centre!" he declared. "There's room for a museum and a café and a video room! It's in a great place! Exactly right!"

He looked around at all the blank faces staring at him.

"I know it's a wacky idea!" Still no one said anything. "But I mean, we should do it up. Mend the windows. Paint it. I could do that! Build an extension. Get a freezer and a fridge, and someone to serve drinks and snacks, and put up a big video screen..." The idea grew even as he spoke, and his imagination conjured up a cool new centre, full of interested holidaymakers, exclaiming over the fascinations of the Scottish west coast. "And we could have a hands-on display, stuff that you can feel and smell and—"

"Isn't it a bit near the Deer Park visitors' centre?" Graeme said slowly.

"Not really. The Deer Park is inland, the other side of the Old Town. And their video is about deer and the Great Caledonian Pine Forest, and how there used to be wolves. This would be about now – the sea birds and seals and fish, and the rocks and gemstones that make up the cliffs and the beach. And anyway, this one would be ours. It would belong to the village."

"Come on, Steve, back down to earth," his dad joked. "You should be a fiction writer specialising in fairy tales!"

"Hang on though, Alan," Mr Campbell interrupted him. "A little enthusiasm goes a long way. It would create jobs, and it would be a tremendous morale booster for the village."

"It might attract more tourists to the area," Amanda added. "My aunty Carrie and uncle Joe used to do bed and breakfast, but they didn't get enough trade."

"They ought to get a web site," Graeme suggested. "Advertise the accommodation and all the tourist attractions of the area."

"A web site!" Amanda exclaimed, her blue eyes wide. "They haven't even got a computer!"

"I think doing up the lifeboat station is a great idea, Steven," said Lucy, her red ponytail bobbing up and down in her excitement. "I could do some of the painting. We could put up posters and make bird tables and—"

"Time to move on," Steven's dad insisted, gathering the children together and herding them along the beach towards the road and the bus stop. Mrs MacKenzie chatted with the girls about polishing gemstones and making them into earrings and bracelets. Mr Campbell caught up with Steven's dad, and Steven stayed close to eavesdrop on their conversation.

"It's an idea. There's always been a wealth of wildlife off Westerley Point. I could put it to the village council, Alan. They meet next week. Why are you so against it?"

"Well, it's just that the kids get so excited about things. Graeme may be tall, and he's bright, but he's younger than our Steven. And Steve himself is such a bundle of energy. Goes a bit overboard." He lowered his voice, and Steven strained to hear. "I just don't want them to get all their hopes up and then be disappointed."

"Yes, well, I take your point. But let's at least give the council chance to think about it. It would have to be a real earner. It would need a lot of finance, not just the sort of makeover the kids might have in mind. No. A real community project. The village could do with a facelift, you know."

"Yeah. OK, Sandy. Thanks. I've been a bit busy, lately, what with my boss being in hospital..."

"Your boss?"

"Yes. My colleague, Rhoda Granderton. She leaves many of the decisions to me nowadays, but she still owns the caravan site. We've known her for so long, she's like one of the family. The kids call her Mrs Granny."

"Yes, I know Rhoda, but I had no idea she was in hospital," Sandy said, shocked.

"Pneumonia. She's going to be OK, but she gave us all a scare. But while she was out of action, and I was away on business overnight, her distant cousin, Jonathan Curtis, took the law into his own hands and moved a JCB on to the site to cut down the trees on the high ground, even though he knew it was against Rhoda's wishes."

"Aye, I heard about that. Quite a shady character, wasn't he?"

"You bet. Bit of a mystery, Jonathan Curtis. Acted on his own most of the time. Funny, really. He turned up out of the blue in the first place, with his wife and his son, Alexander, same age as Steven, and now they seem to have disappeared off the face of the earth."

"Your Steven saved the day though, didn't he?"

"Yes, he did, and there was no harm done. But I guess that's why I didn't want another project just now!"

Steven dropped back and fell into step with Graeme. He started to laugh. "What's up?" Graeme demanded.

"Dad didn't want me to go overboard! Get it? With the lifeboat station. Overboard!" And they both giggled.

Chapter 2
Council decisions

"Lucy?"

"Yeah?"

"What time is it?" Steven was riding in smaller and smaller figures of eight round the back yard of the cottage. He knew he'd asked the time at least three times in the last five minutes, but each time he hoped it was half an hour.

"Steve, find something to do." It was Mum's voice.

"But Sandy Campbell said he'd come round on Saturday morning," Steven complained. "And it is Saturday morning."

"But it's only ten past nine," Mum pointed out. "Most normal people would be in their beds at ten past nine on a Saturday morning."

"Well, I'm not!" Steven replied.

"That's what I said. Most normal people!"

"Mum!"

Mum laughed. "I know you can't wait to hear the village council's verdict, love, but time will pass more quickly if you find something to do. Why don't you go for a bike ride?"

"But I want to be here in case he comes!" Steven explained.

At that moment, a car pulled up in the lane outside the caravan site. "Yeah!" Lucy and Steven shouted. "It's him!"

Sandy Campbell went inside, sat down and stretched his long legs under the kitchen table. Mum made him a cup of coffee. "You're out and about early for a Saturday, Sandy," she commented.

"Nice day. Things to do," he grinned. "Anyway, I figured certain people would be waiting to hear the council's verdict."

"You bet!" Mum smiled. "Put them out of their misery, Sandy."

"It's good news, kids," Sandy grinned. "The council members were impressed with the idea, especially when they heard it came from a youngster – our local hero, in fact!"

Steven felt proud, but he couldn't help blushing. "So what happens next, Mr Campbell?"

"The council reckoned that when the village hear about it, they'd be really enthusiastic, but we need to be sure. It's no good if people say 'Yeah, great,' but do nothing about it. So there's going to be a competition."

"A competition?" Lucy repeated, dancing around the kitchen table.

"Yes. To work out how much support there really is. Everyone is invited to put forward their proposals for raising money for renovating the old lifeboat station, and begin to put them into practice. It was Jimmy Johnstone's idea. He was very keen to get involved. Says he needs a project, now he's retired from teaching. He suggested the best idea should win a prize."

"But who will decide what is the best idea?" Mum asked, frowning.

"It'll probably be the idea that raises the most

money," Sandy explained. "As many ideas as possible will be put into practice, and if people come forward with their suggestions, and join in with other people's ideas, we'll consider the venture a success, and the project will get started."

"So what do we do first?" Steven asked.

"Write down your ideas for raising money. As many as you can think of. Explain them in as much detail as you can. Then hand in the paper to any village council member."

"Can we give them to you?" Lucy asked.

"Yes, of course. Or Mr Johnstone. He's on the village council now he's retired, and he lives just down the road."

"Come on, Steve!" Lucy urged. "Let's tell Graeme. And let's start on our list!" She grabbed her notebook and a biro and the two of them dashed out of the back door.

"Thanks Mr Campbell!" Steven called.

"You're welcome, son," Sandy Campbell replied with a grin.

Graeme saw Steven and Lucy through his caravan window long before they arrived at the caravan. Steven gave him a double thumbs-up sign. Graeme leapt out of the caravan and ran to meet them.

"Did Sandy Campbell come round? Are we on? What did he say?"

"We'll explain it all. We're going up to the Reach to make some plans." So Graeme grabbed his jacket and told his parents where he was off to.

At the high ground at the top of the caravan site they paused as always to look at the strip of blue-grey sea shimmering in the distance, and to drink in the huge expanse of countryside, already showing signs of spring crops. Lucy patted the ground with her hand. "It's dry," she announced. "Let's sit down and make a list." They told Graeme exactly what Sandy Campbell had said.

"So we've got to be able to make a start on the ideas ourselves," Graeme repeated, checking what they had said. "So we mustn't make them too wacky." He screwed up his face, thinking.

"How about a talent contest?" Lucy suggested.

"What? Sing and dance?" Steven pulled a face.

"You wouldn't have to enter, silly! But some of the kids in the Holiday Club love doing that kind of thing. I bet Amanda would enter. She's a fantastic singer! And Mr MacKenzie could do his magic tricks."

"That's a good idea, Lucy," Graeme said. "Write it all down. The mums and dads and grandparents would all come to watch the kids perform."

"What about a craft competition for people who prefer making things instead of performing?" Steven suggested.

"What sort of craft?" Lucy asked.

"Anything! I'd make a bird box. A carved wooden nesting box, with my tools."

"You could enter your wildlife scrapbook, Lucy," Graeme suggested.

"What about you, Graeme?" Steven asked.

"I'd design a poster on the computer, and print it off."

"Yeah! And the grown-ups could do sewing and pottery and stuff," Lucy said enthusiastically, writing as fast as she could.

By mid-morning they had four or five items on

their list, and Lucy announced that she wanted to go back to the cottage to write it out neatly. So in the afternoon, Steven and Graeme got out their bikes and cycled round to Mr Johnstone's, to post it through his letterbox.

When they arrived, there was a man working in the front garden. "Hello, lads!" he said, straightening up and leaning on his spade. "What can I do for you?"

"Are you Mr Johnstone?" Graeme asked. Steven recognised him vaguely.

Mr Johnstone saluted. "At your service!" he replied with a twinkle in his eye. Graeme explained why they'd come.

"Ah! You must be the two boys who came up with the idea of renovating the old lifeboat station at Westerley Point?"

"Yes, well, it was Steven actually," Graeme admitted.

"An excellent idea, boys. Just what the village needs. I'd be pleased to put your fund-raising ideas to the council. We're meeting again next week." He took the envelope from Graeme, and the two of them cycled back to the cottage, very pleased with themselves.

Steven felt very flat on Monday morning when Graeme's family packed their car, closed up their caravan and set off home to Manchester for the start of the new school term on Tuesday. He stood looking down the empty lane long after their car had rounded the bend and disappeared.

"Cheer up, Steve," Dad said, appearing from the cottage garden with an armful of papers, and heading towards Reception. "They'll be back in the summer, maybe even for the half-term break."

But the summer holidays seemed a lifetime away, even though the spring sun carried a hint of warmth, and the evenings stayed light till quite late. Steven just nodded. If Alexander was here, he might cycle or do woodwork with him. "Dad, isn't there any news of the Curtises?" he asked.

"Not a thing. Vanished into thin air."

Steven sighed. "Important term coming up at school, Steve," Dad was continuing. "Last term before starting at high school." Steven nodded again. He didn't want to think about school until he had to, even though he quite enjoyed it when he got there.

"Mrs Granny's coming home from hospital later today," Dad said.

"Oh!" Steven jumped. "Why didn't you tell me?"

"I am telling you!" Dad chuckled. "She phoned a few minutes ago to say the doctor had given her the OK. Last time we visited her, I promised the nurse we'd keep an eye on her."

"I'll keep an eye on her, Dad! I can do that! I'll take meals round for her, and sweep the path for her, and keep her company..."

"You'll have to be careful not to exhaust her!" Dad warned. "Why don't you go and ask Mum if there's anything you could do to get the house ready? Lucy's making a 'welcome home' card. We can all sign it."

So Steven and Mum went across to the site owner's house and left the card on the table, with a small bowl of fruit and a vase of flowers.

Dad went to the hospital in the late afternoon to give Mrs Granny a lift home. When he arrived back at the caravan site, he tooted the horn so that Mum, Steven and Lucy could come out of the cottage to wave.

At teatime, Steven and Lucy went over to the house to invite Mrs Granny to eat with them. She was still very thin, but her cheeks were a bit pinker than last time Steven had seen her, and the old familiar twinkle was back in her eye.

"Hello, dears!" she smiled, giving them each a quick hug. "It's so nice to be home! I had begun to think I wouldn't see the old place again!"

With Mrs Granny back, everything seemed right again. Even though she was not much taller than him, and old enough to be his real grandmother, Steven felt safe, somehow, with Mrs Granny around. Perhaps it was because he had known her all his life, and because she always knew the right thing to do.

"Mum says pneumonia is very serious, Mrs Granny," Lucy said solemnly.

"Yes dear, she's right. But I'm grateful I didn't have anything even more serious. The Lord must want me to stick around a bit longer down here!"

"Mum asked if you want to come and eat with us," Steven told her.

"We're having spaghetti bolognese," Lucy added.

"Well, I love spaghetti bolognese, as you know, but I think I'll just stay here and have a boiled egg and a piece of toast after all the excitement of coming home!" Mrs Granny replied. She sat in her favourite armchair and looked round her living room, smiling. "Sit down and tell me what's been happening," she invited them. So Lucy sat on the floor beside her and Steven sat on the sofa.

"You should have heard Steven give a speech from the shovel of the JCB!" Lucy told her. "He was brilliant, and Graeme's dad could hardly stop everyone clapping and cheering at the end!"

"I'm really sorry to have missed that, Steven. People say you've been the talk of the village ever since! What did you say?"

"I can't really remember," Steven admitted. He felt a bit embarrassed talking about it. "Er, I told them how we'd be destroying wildlife habitats if we developed Hooper's Reach. Anyway, I got all the information from Lucy's wildlife scrapbook. I had the whole night to think about it! When I climbed into the shovel in the evening, I did it just to stop the workmen using the JCB. I couldn't think what else to do. But after I'd read Lucy's book, and after I'd prayed, it all became clear. I told them about the red squirrels, and the badgers, and about all the old trees in the Great Caledonian Pine Forest.

"At the end, Graeme's dad helped. He's a lawyer, and he made everyone see Mr Curtis was in the wrong."

Mrs Granny patted Steven on the shoulder. "Good work, Steven. You're a brave man. If you hadn't—"

"Where did the Curtises go, Mrs Granny?" Lucy interrupted.

"I don't know, dear. That's a mystery to all of us. Mrs Curtis had been saying that if Jonathan's business ventures didn't work, they'd be moving on. But I never suspected it would be so sudden, or that they wouldn't leave a forwarding address.

I imagine they've gone back to the States."

"Mr Curtis was wrong though, wasn't he?" Lucy insisted.

"Yes, he was, but don't tar the whole family with the same brush." Steven looked up, puzzled. Mrs Granny smiled. "What I mean is, even if Jonathan Curtis went about things in the wrong way, it doesn't mean his wife and son were just as bad. I was beginning to think Alexander was a good lad. Thoughtful. Like you, Steven."

No one spoke for a moment, and Mrs Granny looked out of the window, up towards Hooper's Reach. Then she added, "I'd have loved an opportunity to tell Jonathan that it's only people who think that money and success are important. God's more interested in our thoughts and plans." She paused, then said briskly, "Come on now, you two. You'd better go and tell your mum that I'm not coming to eat with you today."

"You'll come soon though, eh?" Lucy asked, jumping up. She gave Mrs Granny a big kiss on the cheek.

"I'd love to, dear."

"Oh, and er, Mrs Granny? Dad says if you hear from the Curtises, would you let him know?" Steven added.

"Of course, but I was going to say the same thing to him! Bye dear. Thank you so much for coming round."

Chapter 3
Planning ahead

Steven was glad when the first two or three days of the new school term were over, and the comments about his night in the JCB seemed to have dried up.

Arriving home from school one afternoon, he found Dad and Lucy talking to Sandy Campbell in the back yard of the cottage. "Sure!" Dad was saying. "I'll see what I can do. I'll start with Farmer MacKay. He's got a number of trailers and heavy-duty vehicles. I'm sure he'll help us out."

"Thanks, Alan," Sandy replied. "Oh, hi, Steven! How's school?"

"Fine, thanks, Mr Campbell. Dad, what are you going to ask Farmer MacKay for?"

Dad smiled. "Steve, meet the Project General Co-ordinator!"

"The what?" Steven asked, looking from one to the other of them.

"The General Co-ordinator!" Lucy repeated proudly.

"Ever since we started," Dad explained, "Sandy has shown so much energetic commitment to the project to renovate the old lifeboat station that the village council has asked him to co-ordinate the whole thing!"

"It'll keep me out of mischief," Sandy grinned. "I've given your dad a list of forthcoming events, and he's agreed to help out."

Steven took the list from Dad, and Lucy moved to read it with him. "What a lot of different things!" he exclaimed. "I can't wait to get started!"

"We'd still welcome more ideas, though," Sandy said. "Most of these are one-off events, needing a lot of preparation beforehand, then all over in one afternoon. Take the talent contest, for example, or the half marathon. So if you have any more ideas for ongoing fundraising events which people can enjoy over a period of time, the village council would be very interested."

"You're on, Sandy. You've come to the right place," Dad smiled, looking from Steven to Lucy. "This is your local ideas factory!"

Sandy grinned and got into his car. "Thanks, Alan. Bye kids. See you soon." And he drove off down the lane.

"Let's see the list again, Dad," Steven said, dumping his school bag on the kitchen floor. He and Lucy sat at the table.

"Talent contest, craft competition, car treasure hunt, village sports day..." Lucy read out.

"There won't be enough Saturdays in July for all those," Dad remarked.

"Some are in June," Steven told him, looking at the dates. "And some are on Fridays."

"Parade," Lucy read. "What's the parade?"

"That was Sandy's idea," Dad explained. "He's asked all the clubs and societies in the village to decorate a float, and they're all going to drive slowly around the neighbourhood in a long procession."

"What kind of float?" Lucy asked.

"A van, or trailer, with people standing, or sitting, or acting, advertising their society, and asking for money for the project," Dad explained. "And if everyone in the village comes to watch, and we drive around the Old Town, the New Town and the neighbouring villages, we can collect money as we go. I promised to see about transport for it."

"Sounds great, Dad!" Lucy declared. "Wonder what we can do for it?"

"And what could we suggest that wouldn't all happen on one day?" Steven wondered. "Like Sandy suggested; we need a different kind of idea."

There was a knock at the back door. Steven looked up, surprised. Most people just walked in and called "Hello!" Amanda was standing shyly on the doorstep.

"Hi!" said Steven, suddenly tongue-tied.

"Invite her in, then!" Dad said, laughing.

"Oh, er, sorry. Come in." He pulled a chair up to the table for her.

"Thanks. Er, Mr MacKenzie sent me to ask you for some help. You know Mr Campbell's had this idea of a parade at the end of July?"

"Yes," Dad said slowly. "He's asked me to rustle up some transport."

"Great!" Amanda said.

"Transport for what?" Mum asked, arriving at the back door with a bundle of letters from Reception. "Hello, dear," she said to Amanda, pulling up a chair and joining everyone at the kitchen table.

"The parade, Mum," Lucy said, her eyes shining. "Lots of village clubs are going to drive round and collect money for the project."

"Which groups are joining in?" Mum asked.

"Just about everyone," Amanda replied. "There's the drama club, and the football team, and the Young Farmers' group, the Scouts and Guides, the tennis club, the rambling club, even the flower arranging club! And I suggested to Mr MacKenzie that we should do a Holiday Club float."

"That's a great idea!" Lucy agreed. "Can I be on it?"

"What sort of float is it going to be?" Mum asked.

"Well, that's what I came to ask… er, that is, if you've got any ideas," Amanda finished.

"We should get lots of the Holiday Club kids to ride on it," Steven suggested. "I mean, the little ones."

"They could act something. A Bible story!"

"One of the stories Mr MacKenzie told at Easter!"

"David and Goliath! The smallest children could be sheep."

"I'm sure the costumes we made must be hidden away somewhere!" The ideas came thick and fast, and everyone chipped in.

"Who could be David?"

"And who could be Goliath?"

"Steven, you could be David," Mum suggested.

"Ugh!" Steven groaned. "I'd rather help to set it up. I'd hate to ride around all day wearing a tea towel on my head and with everyone staring at me! What are you going to be, Amanda?" he asked, trying to change the subject.

"I'm not sure yet."

"Don't you think there should be other things, as well as the Bible story?" Dad suggested. "To show what a wide variety of things you do at the Holiday Club?"

"If we had other things, I'd be an artist!" Lucy announced. "What do artists wear?"

"They wear blue smock overalls, and carry a paintbrush and a palette!" Mum told her.

"If you go as an artist, I'll go as a footballer!" Amanda declared.

"Yeah," Steven agreed, enthusiasm suddenly bubbling up inside him. "We could have four activity corners, with a Bible story being acted out in the middle."

"We're going to need a very big vehicle for all this," Dad observed.

"Mr MacGregor, would you be Goliath?" Amanda asked.

"Yes, Dad!" Lucy pleaded, jumping up and down. "We could make you some tin foil armour!"

Dad and Mum exchanged glances. "You know your dad," Mum told Steven and Lucy. "He doesn't even like wearing a tie, never mind dressing up and having people looking at him."

Steven considered his dad for a moment. Suddenly, he understood him exactly. Not everybody liked to be stared at. Some people just preferred to get on with a job. "I know just how you feel, Dad," he reassured him.

"I think I should drive the tractor and trailer!" Dad said, breathing a sigh of relief.

"Well, Dad, you have to dress up," Lucy insisted. "You can't just wear your usual jeans and check shirt. It's too boring."

"Mrs MacGregor!" Amanda said suddenly. "Would you be Goliath?"

"Me? I'm not tall enough!" Mum laughed.

"You're taller than me!" Amanda objected.

"And me!" Lucy and Steven chipped in.

"Well, love, if Shakespeare had men actors to act his women's parts, I'm sure we could have a female Goliath!" Dad laughed. "You'd be taller than the little kids – the sheep. And we could find someone small to be David."

"That's a good start, anyway!" Amanda said, standing up. "Thanks very much."

"Well done, Amanda," Mum said warmly.

"Tell Mr MacKenzie I'll see Farmer MacKay about the trailer," Dad added.

"Thanks, Mr MacGregor. And, er..."

"What dear?" Mum asked.

"Mrs MacGregor, please persuade Mr MacGregor to wear a costume when he drives the trailer. It would be much more fun!" And Amanda skipped out with a grin, before anyone could refuse.

"Let me see the programme," Mum said. "Goodness, everyone's going to be busy!"

Dad peered over her shoulder. "The first Saturday in August is going to be the big one," he commented. "The half marathon, with the prize giving at the end."

"The parade will be a big one, too," Mum groaned. "Better get planning. What are you up to, Lucy?"

"I'm making a countdown calendar to my favourite events," she announced. She had taken the calendar down from the kitchen wall, and she was writing numbers on three little blocks of coloured paper – green, yellow and pink.

"Ninety-eight? Why are you starting from the back?" Steven asked.

"Because it's a countdown!" she told him with exaggerated patience. "It's ninety-eight days till the prize giving, then tomorrow it'll be ninety-seven, then ninety-six, and so on! I'll peel one ticket off each day. But I've got four favourite events, and only three colours," she complained.

"Use just one colour for the craft competition and the talent contest," Mum told her. "They're on the same day."

So Steven counted ninety-one days to the parade, and seventy to the craft competition and the talent contest.

"Well, if it's only ninety-one days to the parade, I'd better go and visit Farmer MacKay straight away to talk about transport!" Dad announced.

"But Dad, it's..." Steven began. Then he noticed a twinkle in his dad's eye. He was teasing, because Lucy always got so carried away.

"Bye, Dad," he grinned.

Chapter 4

A surprise appearance

As April gave way to May the evenings were long and light, and Steven loved to spend time at Hooper's Reach in his hide, looking out for birds he hadn't spotted last year. Eventually, the bird box he was making as his entry for the craft competition would go up there. He could see it in his mind's eye, nailed high in a tree, where he could watch blue tits go in and out. According to Lucy's countdown blocks, there were still fifty-six days to go, and he had made a good start. There was no rush.

But one evening, he found someone had put up a makeshift bird table at the edge of the woodland area, near his hide. He felt puzzled and indignant. The table was roughly made, with nails sticking out at odd angles, and it wasn't quite level. As soon as there's a breeze, Steven thought scornfully, everything will blow off. But it was well stocked with nuts and bacon rind.

Back at the cottage, he asked, "Dad, do you know who put the bird table up at Hooper's Reach?"

"Bird table? No, son. No idea. I shouldn't have thought the birds would need it just now. It's in wintertime that the birds need help to find food."

"I know," Steven agreed. "It's just a couple of pieces of wood nailed together, but someone keeps it topped up. I think the grey squirrels eat most of the stuff."

"Let's be detectives and find out who it is!" Lucy said enthusiastically.

But they didn't need to try very hard because the following evening as Steven was waiting silently in his hide, hoping to see a green woodpecker, he heard someone walking up the path between the caravans, whistling. He was just about to come out and say hello, when he froze in amazement. It was Alexander Curtis! He had a small polythene bag full of food, and he'd come to refill the bird table. Steven thought his eyes were playing tricks on him! He wondered if this boy just looked like Alexander. He was so sure by now that the Curtises were in America. How could Alexander be here, at Hooper's Reach?

For a moment, Steven couldn't decide what to do. He was tempted to jump out and frighten the wits out of Alexander, but uncomfortable memories of the unkind tricks that he, Lucy and Graeme had played on Alexander before somehow stopped him.

So instead, Steven just shuffled a bit, and trod on a couple of crackly twigs before emerging from his hide and saying, "Hi!"

Alexander grinned. "Hi! I was hoping you'd come."

"I thought you'd gone back to America!"

"My dad has, but Mom and I are living in the village again."

"In the village? Where?"

"In a bed-sitting room above Mitchells', the newsagents."

34

"What, you and your mum?" Steven couldn't imagine Anne-Marie Curtis and Alexander in a bed-sit. He could only imagine them in a posh, spacious house like the ones on American films.

"Yeah," Alexander admitted.

"Where's your mum just now?"

"She's got a part-time job helping Mr Mitchell in the shop."

"But..." Something didn't sound quite right, but Steven couldn't work out what it was. "Does Mrs Granny know you're back?"

"Not yet. But Mom and I are planning to visit soon. Is she better?"

"Yes. She took it easy for a while, and my mum took meals round. But she's properly back at work now."

"Great! Look, I gotta go now. Will you be coming up here tomorrow?"

"Could do. But what about—"

"Great!" Alexander said again. "I'll see you tomorrow then." And he ran off down the steep path between the caravans.

"Dad! Mum!" Steven shouted, bursting in through the back door of the cottage. Dad and Lucy were in the kitchen, and Mum came running down the stairs.

"What's happened, love?" Mum asked anxiously.

Steven grinned for a moment at their worried faces. "The Curtises are back! At least, Alexander and his mum are."

"Are you sure? How do you know?" Dad asked.

"Alexander was up at the Reach. It was him who put up the bird table."

"Are they back at Mrs Granny's?" Lucy asked.

"No, they're staying in a bed-sit above Mr Mitchell's shop."

"What?" Mum and Dad said together.

"Mrs Curtis is working in the shop," Steven added.

"So where's Jonathan?" Dad asked, looking puzzled.

"Gone back to the States, I think," Steven replied.

"Does Mrs Granny know?" Mum asked.

"No, I don't think so, because Alexander asked if she was better, so they can't have visited her yet."

"Anyway, she'd have said something," Mum reasoned, looking as puzzled as Dad. "I think we'd better go round and tell her, then try to find out what's happening. Sounds like something's gone wrong for them."

It wasn't till Steven was in bed that Dad came back from Mrs Granny's. Steven shot out of bed and downstairs when he heard Dad's voice.

"You not asleep yet, Steve?"

"What did Mrs Granny say, Dad? Did she know?"

"No, she had no idea. Thought they were back in the States. But we agreed that we need to get in touch with Mrs Curtis. Mum says she'll go round to the newsagents tomorrow and invite Alexander and his mum round here. They could eat with us tomorrow evening. Mum's invited Mrs Granny, too. So we'll probably get the whole story then. Now, off to bed, nosy parker!"

"Hi everybody!" Mrs Curtis stood at the back door of the cottage the following evening, smiling. She was as pretty as ever, but there was something different though Steven couldn't quite decide what it was. Maybe she was a bit paler than usual. Alexander stood behind her. Steven thought they looked a bit shy. He felt a bit shy himself, though he didn't quite know why.

"Come on in," Mum said, opening the door wide. She gave Mrs Curtis a peck on the cheek.

Mrs Granny gave her a hug, and ruffled Alexander's hair. "Well! I'm sure you've grown," she told him, "even in these few weeks."

"It's your good Scottish porridge!" Mrs Curtis joked. "But how about you, Rhoda? We left in such a hurry, and you were so..."

"I'm fine now, thanks. Bad bout of pneumonia. Gave everyone a scare. But thanks to Alan and Jane's good care I'm back on top." She put a hand on each of Mum and Dad's shoulders as she spoke, and Steven thought everyone was a bit stiff. On their best behaviour.

"Alexander!" Lucy said suddenly. "Your woodwork's not very good! You'll have to get Steven to teach you how to use the tools! He can—"

"Lucy!" Mum and Dad exploded together. "Don't be rude!"

"That bird table was perfectly all right," Mum began.

"It's OK, Mrs MacGregor," Alexander said, still smiling. "I'm not very good with tools yet, but I sure would like to get better!" He turned to Mrs Granny. "Thank you for the tools, Aunt Rhoda."

"He's always wanted his own tools," Mrs Curtis added. "He had his eye on that box under the stairs in your house."

"I'm delighted you found my note and were able to take them with you," Mrs Granny beamed.

"Come on, everyone – dinner-time!" Mum announced. So they all squashed around the table in the kitchen and Mum served a delicious meal. Gradually everyone relaxed, and before they'd finished eating, everything seemed back to normal. Better than normal, Steven thought, because Jonathan Curtis wasn't there. He was the one who used to spoil things. Mrs Curtis and Alexander were different. More easy-going. It was only Mr Curtis who was so bossy and wanted to change everything. Steven really began to enjoy himself. These were some of his favourite people.

"Well, I guess I'd better tell you what we're doing back here, since you're all too polite to ask outright!" Mrs Curtis said hesitantly as they were finishing their pudding. "It's a long story, so I hope you're sitting comfortably!

"When we first came over here, Jonathan really wanted to, er, kinda seek his fortune, like Dick Whittington in the old rhyme. Only he wanted to come to Scotland, instead of London, because his ancestors came from the west coast, too."

"We always thought his business in the US had gone really well," Dad said.

"It did, at first," Mrs Curtis agreed. "He was working with his cousin, Will. See, Will was an architect, and Jonathan headed up a building firm. They were a good partnership, at first. Then Will got divorced, and he owed his ex-wife a lot of money, and he started pushing Jonathan to work harder, and began to demand a bigger share from the partnership. He said Jonathan was completely dependent on him. No plans, no building! So I guess he was right. Sort of." She pushed her chair back a little and took a deep breath.

"He must have been exhausted, working all hours," Mrs Granny put in.

"Yes, he was, Rhoda, he was."

"And grumpy!" Alexander added.

"Now, Alexander," Mrs Curtis warned. "It was very hard for him. But in the end, his foreman came up with an idea that looked like speeding everything up. And it did, at first. It was only later that we found it had meant cutting corners, such as safety measures. But then there was a fire, and that's how they discovered how much had been left out."

"Was anyone hurt?" Mum asked anxiously.

"No, fortunately. It happened at night. But if everything had been done correctly, it wouldn't have happened."

"Wow!" Mum breathed. Everyone was silent for a moment, thinking. "Let me get some coffee before you go on." She got up and put the kettle on. Steven began to realise that Jonathan Curtis had been into something really serious.

Lucy must have realised, too, because she asked, "Did Mr Curtis's firm have to pay for all the damage, then?"

"Well, honey," Mrs Curtis explained, "legally, he and his cousin Will had to share it. It was in the rules of the partnership. And it wasn't the fault of either of them personally, but they were both responsible." She paused, and Steven thought she looked really miserable.

"There was a huge row," Alexander explained. "And Dad said he wouldn't ever work with Uncle

Will again. Anyway, it was all Uncle Will's fault in the first place…"

"Alexander!" his mother warned him again. Then she looked round the table at everyone. Steven looked round, too. They all looked sad and shocked. "We agreed we weren't going to start blaming people because it really doesn't help," Mrs Curtis continued. She paused while Mum put mugs of coffee in front of the grown-ups and passed the milk and sugar round.

"But where is Mr Curtis now?" Steven asked. He'd been waiting for this part of the story, and he just felt he couldn't wait any longer.

"He's back home trying to sort our money out, honey," Mrs Curtis replied. "Once the legal stuff was fixed, Will had control of the company finances, including Jonathan's share. But there's an even worse bit to come, and since you guys are all being so good to us, it's only fair that you know it all."

"Don't worry, Anne-Marie," Mrs Granny said, putting a hand on Mrs Curtis's arm. "We're glad to have you two back here safely, and we only want the best for him, too."

"When we left here and, well, it was all a bit sudden, you know." She stirred her coffee round and round, and took a moment before she could continue. "Jonathan knew he was out of order trying to push the developments through without your say-so, Rhoda. But, well, he really thought it was best for you and the caravan site."

"But we tried to persuade him that it wasn't really the best thing," Alexander interrupted. "See, we've always lived in big cities before, and he couldn't understand villages. But me and Mom, we really like it here. Villages are neat!"

"I'm afraid we did have a couple of arguments about it," Mrs Curtis admitted. "But I think it was because he'd seen one project fail, he wanted to push another one through successfully as quickly as possible. He just couldn't wait."

"Then Graeme's dad got involved," Alexander added.

"Yeah," Mrs Curtis added. "When he saw that it was all in the hands of lawyers again, he really freaked out. Insisted that we left right away. The only good thing about it was that you were in hospital, Rhoda."

"That wasn't good!" Steven objected.

"No, what I mean is, honey, that your Mrs Granny was in good hands, with doctors to look after her," she told Steven. Then she turned to Mrs Granny. "I wished I'd insisted earlier that you went to the doctor again. I'd have refused to leave with Jonathan if you'd needed us, Rhoda."

Mrs Granny patted her arm again. "I was a stubborn old thing," she admitted, "but God works all things together for good."

"Well, it's really good that you're well again, Aunt Rhoda," Alexander said.

"But here comes the worst bit," Mrs Curtis continued, taking a deep breath. "Jonathan was fed up. Really depressed, and angry. We drove into Glasgow, looking for somewhere to stay for a night or two while we made decisions. And Jonathan had a couple of drinks. Not enough to be drunk. But enough to blow all our money in a casino."

"A what?" Lucy asked.

"A casino – where people play gambling games, honey. They bet a lot of money that they'll win a game, and if they win they're rich. But if they lose, they have to pay up."

"And Mr Curtis lost?" Steven asked.

"You guessed it. He lost a lot of money. Almost all we had, although that wasn't much. Funny thing is, in the morning, when he was dead sober, he could remember everything real clearly, and he said the establishment wasn't run properly. Said the managers were cheating."

"How did he know?" Dad asked.

"I'm not sure, Alan. Only, he's been to casinos before, back home in the States, and he understands the organisation. So he challenged them, and they got the bouncers in and threatened to throw him out."

"Wow!" Steven breathed. "What did he do?"

"Fortunately, he had the sense to go. Otherwise I dread to think what they might have done to him. He said he was going to file a complaint."

"And then?" Mum asked.

"Then he decided he'd have to go back and sort things out with Will. It was the only possibility he had," Mrs Curtis concluded.

"So you stayed in Glasgow?" Mrs Granny asked.

"For a while, yes. We lived in a bed and breakfast place."

"But it was so boring," Alexander put in.

"And lonely," Mrs Curtis added. "Jonathan thought we ought to stay in Glasgow. More anonymous. He thought no one could track us down in a big city."

"Track you down?" Mrs Granny repeated.

"Oh, Jonathan gets a bit hyper about things. He thought people from the casino might come hunting for him. But you can feel so alone in a city. We really missed the village."

"And haven't you been to school?" Lucy asked Alexander.

"I've been doing a home-school course," Alexander explained. "But I think I'd rather go to school."

"You could come with us!" Lucy said with enthusiasm. "You'd probably be in Steve's class."

"Yeah! I'd like that! Mom?" Alexander turned to his mother.

"We'll see about that, honey."

"I'll take you and introduce you to the head teacher if you like," Steven's mum suggested.

"In the meantime," Mrs Granny interrupted, "There's more than enough room for you at the house, as you know. I don't like to think of the two of you confined to one room while I've got spare bedrooms, and there's lots of—"

"Wow! Can we, Mom?" Alexander's eyes were shining.

"Rhoda, that's a wonderfully kind offer, but I really don't think we should—"

"I was looking forward to some of your delicious cookies," Mrs Granny interrupted. "And there's lots of work to do on the site now that the season's in full swing. We could do with an extra pair of hands." She looked expectantly at Mrs Curtis.

"Well, if you're sure..."

"Sure, I'm sure!" Mrs Granny beamed. "It's a deal! Pack up your things and move back in as soon as you can."

"Great!" Steven agreed. "We could use the tools and I could show you how to choose the right sized bit for the drill. We could make a level bird table."

Alexander grinned.

Chapter 5
Down to business

It was fun having Alexander living in Mrs Granny's house again, and in the same class at school. Steven was given the job of showing him round and explaining everything to him while he settled in. He'd only been there a week when the school closed for half-term.

On the first day of the holiday, Alexander appeared in the yard on his bike. Steven went out to join him, and they rode up and down the lane, which was dappled with sunlight filtering through the trees.

"Could we get your go-kart out?" Alexander asked.

"The Silver Cloud? Um, trouble is," Steven explained, "it doesn't have any brakes, so I usually only use it in the winter, when the site's deserted. In the summer, when there are people walking around, I use my bike."

"But there's that track," Alexander suggested, "the one that goes down beyond the far side of Mrs Granny's house. We could use that!"

"OK," Steven agreed. He was as keen to take out the Silver Cloud as Alexander was.

"Do you remember when you told me to get out of the way of your landing stage?"

"And you laughed at me?"

"Yeah, and you wrestled me." They both laughed. It was good to remember without any hard feelings.

"Then Mrs Granny came out into her garden, and we both felt guilty," Steven recalled.

"Yeah. I reckon she knew what was going on, even though all she said was, 'Come and wash your hands for lunch'!"

Steven said, "Come on. The Silver Cloud's in our shed."

"Why do you call it the Silver Cloud?" Alexander asked.

"It was the name of one of the early Rolls Royce cars. Very fast and posh. Hey!" He stopped in his tracks in amazement to see Graeme in the cottage yard. "What are you doing here?" he grinned, delighted.

Graeme looked even more amazed as he stared at Alexander. "What's he doing here?" he asked Steven darkly. "I thought he'd disappeared off the face of the earth!"

"Graeme!" Steven's mum appeared at the back door of the cottage. "How nice to see you. Your mum said you were coming. School mid-term break, is it?"

"Hello, Mrs MacGregor. It's just Mum and me. My dad's got to work."

"Well, come in and have a quick drink of juice, and I'll catch you up on the news." She led Graeme inside, while Steven and Alexander took the Silver Cloud carefully out of the shed.

When Graeme came outside again five minutes later he was smiling, and he spoke to Alexander like a long lost pal. Good old Mum, thought Steven. She's explained it so we can all be friends.

"We're going up to the top of the lane beyond Mrs Granny's," Steven told Graeme. "It's ages since we had the Silver Cloud out. So what's the news?"

"None from my end. It's all at your end," Graeme replied, looking from one to the other. "You should have written to me."

Steven snorted. "I only write cards at Christmas!"

"Well, e-mail, then."

"Haven't got a PC."

"There's one in Reception," Graeme reminded them.

"Can't type." It was the last thing Steven could imagine doing, sitting still in front of a keyboard and screen. He didn't even particularly enjoy computer games, though he played them with his school friends on wet days. He'd always rather be outside, working with wood and nails, or plumbing in a caravan, or helping Dad with site planning.

"Typing's easy," Alexander said.

"Have you got a PC then?" Steven asked.

"Yeah, you bet! A laptop. That's how we keep in contact with my dad."

They had reached the top of the rise, and Steven took the first ride downhill on the Silver Cloud. The other two raced down beside him, shouting warnings about twists and bumps in the lane, and good-naturedly arguing whose turn was next.

"So, how's the competition going then?" Graeme asked, as they pulled the Silver Cloud back up hill.

"What competition?" Alexander asked. So Steven and Graeme explained the visitors' centre idea, and the village council's response.

"We've already given in a list of suggestions, but

the council's accepting more and more all the time," Steven added. "Mr Campbell said we need something that doesn't happen in one afternoon."

"Wish my dad was here," Alexander said wistfully. "He'd be really good at this sort of thing."

"But what would *you* do?" Steven asked, trying to change the subject.

"Well, we have to think what people will pay for," Alexander said. Steven suddenly thought he looked exactly like his dad.

"Hey, it's my go!" Alexander said as they reached the top. And this time it was Steven's turn to run downhill with Graeme while Alexander rode the Silver Cloud. The cool wind on his face and the mad dash filled Steven with enthusiasm for his idea once again, and by the time they walked up hill for the third time he was very eager to hear Alexander's suggestions.

"We could buy a box of colourful T-shirts," Alexander gasped, out of breath. "Really cheap ones, like £5 each. My mum is brilliant at sewing and all that kind of thing. She could embroider a logo on each one, like a famous sports make, and we could sell them for £20 each!"

"Wow!" Graeme grinned. "£15 net gain for each one. At that rate, we could even keep a couple of pounds profit to split between us, and give in £10 profit for each one."

"But wouldn't it be like... like cheating?" Steven objected. "I mean, they wouldn't be the real thing, would they?"

"Those T-shirts are a rip-off anyway," Alexander agreed. "You pay £5 for the shirt and £15 or more for the design, and some of the designs are really small. But my dad says if people are stupid enough to pay for them, the manufacturer deserves his profit."

"Anyway, it's a bit like how you can get a Rolex watch for a fiver in the market in the Far East," Graeme added.

"Only they're not real Rolex watches," Steven pointed out.

"Of course not!" Graeme and Alexander chorused, and they both laughed. Steven joined in.

"And no one forces people to pay it. They just do," Alexander added. "And you remember those fliers you made at Easter, asking people to sign the petition to stop Hooper's Reach being dug up?" he asked, turning to Graeme.

"Yes. I did the computer stuff but Lucy did the drawing."

"Yeah. She's good. Maybe we could make some labels the same way."

"Labels?" Steven asked.

"Yup. Organic foods labels, like it was a real food firm. Then my mom could make some cakes and we could wrap each one in cling film and stick labels on them. Organic foods made with whole food ingredients always sell for much more, at least in the States they do, and I guess it's the same here."

"And does your mum always use organic ingredients?" Steven asked, feeling confused.

"Course not! But she uses good stuff."

"But what if, um, people ask if the ingredients really are organic, or something?" Steven asked.

"They wouldn't," Graeme assured him, "Because everyone's in a good mood about the renovations and stuff. We wouldn't get caught. It's my turn!" he finished, leaping on to the Silver Cloud. "Steve, give me a good push start."

"But it's all, well, not quite honest," Steven said, giving the Silver Cloud a huge shove. Getting caught had never entered his mind. It was something else. He couldn't put it into words.

"We're not forcing anyone to buy things," Graeme shouted over the noise of the Silver Cloud's wheels and Steven and Alexander's pounding feet.

"And it's all in a very good cause," Alexander added, puffing. "An unselfish cause. For the good of the whole village!"

"Remember how Graeme and I tried to trick you and your dad into thinking you couldn't get lighting or plumbing to caravans on the high ground?" Steven reminded him, running beside the go-kart.

"Yeah!"

"And how we pretended the high ground was haunted, to scare you away?"

"I'll never forget it!" Alexander panted. Steven was glad they could put all that behind them, but he wanted to use it to explain. He and Graeme had really scared Alexander, but it was such a mean trick, they'd regretted it later.

"That was in a good cause, too, but..."

"Look out!" Alexander yelled.

Too late! Graeme lost control of the kart and mounted the grass verge at the edge of the lane. He slid along the gravel for a couple of metres with the Silver Cloud on top of him.

"Ow!" he said, righting himself and the go-kart, and examining his grazed knees and elbows. "I'd better go back to the caravan and get cleaned up."

"Tough luck," said Alexander sympathetically. "Steve, can I have one more shot?"

"OK," Steven agreed. "I just have to go and see Mrs Granny about something. Catch you in a minute." So, while Graeme hobbled back to his caravan, and Alexander trudged up the hill a final time, Steven went to Mrs Granny's back door, opened it slowly, and called "Hello!" as usual.

Mrs Granny always had time for people. Especially himself, Steven reflected. They sat at the kitchen table with a glass of lemonade, and he told her about the conversation with Graeme and Alexander. "They were so keen," he said, "and they were working so hard on my idea. And after all, it was all for the good of the village. Even if it wasn't completely honest, it wouldn't be hurting anyone, or actually telling lies."

"But I'm guessing that you didn't feel comfortable with the ideas," Mrs Granny asked.

"No, I didn't. But I can't quite see why."

"Do you still read your Bible each day?" she asked.

"Yes. Well, most days."

"So you're getting to know God more and more, and that includes getting to know what he likes and what he doesn't like."

"I suppose so."

"Well, you're right that those money-raising ideas were not quite honest. They would all involve a bit of lying and cheating. But there's an even more important thing. Would they please God?"

"No, I don't think so," Steven replied.

"I think you're right, and I think you knew that instinctively, even when you couldn't quite explain it. And that's because you're getting to know God. The more you get to know a friend, the more you know what he likes, and what he doesn't like. It's the same with God, you know," Mrs Granny finished, leaning back in her chair.

"I wish I could explain that to Graeme and Alexander," Steven said wistfully.

"You're probably doing more than you realise to show them that Christians are different," Mrs Granny said. "Just keep praying for them, and for Alexander's father, too. Only God can get him out of the mess he's got himself into. It's just as well he left that casino when he did. Those gambling operators don't care. They would think nothing of mugging their customers if they thought they could make more money. From what Mrs Curtis said, I think Jonathan had a near miss."

"Wow!" Steven breathed. It sounded like a gangster film. Even though he didn't like Jonathan Curtis, he didn't want to think he was in real danger. "Yes, I'll keep praying. Thanks, Mrs Granny." Steven drained his glass and ran out of the back door, almost colliding with Alexander and the Silver Cloud.

"Let's go and see if Graeme's all right," Alexander suggested.

"OK. Let's drop off the Silver Cloud at home on the way."

At the cottage, Lucy was at a loose end. "Where are you two going?" she demanded. They explained about Graeme's grazed knees. "I'm coming too," she announced.

Steven opened his mouth to object, but Mum called, "Twenty minutes 'till lunch. Don't be too long." So the three of them walked over to Graeme's caravan. He emerged grinning and showing off sticking plasters on both knees and one elbow.

"We've just got time to walk up to the Reach before Lucy and I have to go home for lunch," Steven said.

At the top of the site, Steven showed Graeme where Alexander had put his bird table, and told him about the bit of detective work he'd done to discover who it was.

"So you'll be around in the summer when we start all the fundraising events?" Graeme asked Alexander.

"Looks like it. But it depends on my dad."

"Well, I think you've got some of your dad's business ideas," Graeme said. "What do you think, Steve? Should we enter some more ideas for the contest?"

"What ideas?" Lucy asked eagerly. So Graeme explained the suggestions that Alexander had put forward.

"But you can't do that!" Lucy objected immediately. "It'd be cheating. Or lying. Or both!"

Steven felt ashamed of himself. Trust Lucy not to mince her words!

"Why?" Graeme and Alexander said together. Alexander added, "We wouldn't be forcing anyone to buy anything. And it's for a good cause."

Lucy looked at Steven. "It's not quite right," he stammered.

"What's not right about creating new jobs for people in the village, or about telling all the visitors how beautiful Scotland is?"

"Well, I just want to get it right," Steven muttered. "I want to... er..."

"He wants to please God!" Lucy declared.

"What?" Graeme and Alexander chorused.

"I want to please God. That's the... er... the most important thing," Steven said, gaining courage.

"Well, how do you know how to do that?" Graeme asked.

"I read the Bible every day, and it's like hearing his... er... instructions." He'd been going to say 'his voice', but he figured it would sound a bit wacky.

"But the Bible's such an old book. It's impossible to understand!" Graeme complained.

"Not if you read a bit at a time, and use a guide or puzzle books. They give you questions and quizzes and things to help you understand..."

"You mean, you reckon you can know what God likes, the way you can know what your teacher likes, because you know him well...?" Graeme began.

"Or what he doesn't like?" Alexander finished.

"Yes!" Lucy agreed eagerly. "It's like getting a personal letter from him every day!"

"Or an e-mail," Steven added, grinning.

They walked thoughtfully back down the hill, and as he and Lucy reached the cottage, Steven said reluctantly, "Thanks, Luce. I didn't know you, er, you..."

"I became a Christian at Holiday Club last year,"

she explained. "I've been reading my Bible for a whole year!"

"Why didn't you tell me?"

"I thought you might tease me."

"Yes, I probably would've," he admitted.

Chapter 6
New talents, new ideas

Steven leapt out of bed and pulled back the curtains. The sun was shining again, and although it wasn't yet seven o'clock he was eager to get up and out. Nevertheless, he forced himself to go back and sit up in bed to read his Bible. He knew that if he didn't do it now, he'd be too busy and forget.

He took out his Bible and his puzzle book, and turned to Matthew chapter 25. Steven recognised Jesus' story immediately. He'd heard it before. A rich man went away and entrusted his money to his servants. He gave the first one 5,000 silver coins. The second got 2,000 silver coins, and the third got 1,000. The rich man told them to put his money to good use. The first two doubled their money, and the rich man was pleased with them, but the third servant buried his money in a hole in the ground. The rich man was very angry and sent him away.

Steven stared out of the window and tried to think hard. "What are you saying to me, Lord?" he prayed. Mrs Granny always said the Bible was like a letter from God, not a book from the library.

The puzzle book said, 'Jesus is like the rich man. He gives us all good things, such as possessions and abilities, and tells us to make good use of them.' On the page was a small space for Steven to draw what he had that he could use for God. But he couldn't think what to draw.

Putting the books down, he went to stand by the window. Gazing up the hill towards the Reach, he prayed, "Lord, how can we make good use of the things you've given us in order to help the lifeboat station project?" He paused for a moment, trying to think. But his mind was blank, so he said "Amen". Then he got dressed as fast as he could, and went downstairs for breakfast.

After breakfast, Steven and Lucy went to collect Graeme from his caravan, and together they went to Mrs Granny's house to call in for Alexander. He was already outside in the garden with the box of tools Mrs Granny had given him, waiting for Steven to show him how to use the drill.

"You'd better watch out, Steve or Alexander will win the craft exhibition, and you'll only come second!" Lucy joked.

Alexander just grinned. "Not much risk of that," he said. "But it's all right for you guys. You were here from the beginning. I wish I'd been here when you gave your list of ideas to the council."

"It's not too late," Lucy said. "What we need to do is to work out what people are good at. Everybody's got talents. Mrs Granny always says so. And if you've got a talent, you shouldn't waste it! You should use it for everybody else's good, not just your own."

"So?" Alexander asked.

"So," she replied importantly, chewing the end of her pencil, "For example, if Graeme is good with computers, he should use that skill for someone else."

"But how would that help the lifeboat station fund?" Steven objected.

"Oh!" Graeme suddenly stood up and dropped the piece of wood he'd been holding for Alexander. "I've just had an idea! We could..." Then he sighed and sat down again.

"What?" the other three asked. "We could what?"

"No, it would never work. It's a stupid idea."

"We'll decide if it's stupid or not. Just tell us," Steven insisted.

"Well, the village doesn't have an Internet café," he said slowly. The others stared at him blankly. "There! I told you it was a stupid idea," he muttered.

"No, no. Wait a minute," Alexander told him. "It's not such a bad idea! In the States, lots of small towns have a community Internet café."

"Have you ever been into one?" Graeme asked eagerly.

"Er, no. But that's because we already have a computer."

"How about you, Graeme?" Steven asked.

"Well, there are lots of Internet cafés in Manchester. But we've already got a computer, too. Like Alexander."

"Well, we haven't," Lucy said. "And Mrs Granny hasn't."

"And Mr Campbell hasn't! He told us!" Steven declared.

"The adults will just say it's too wacky," Graeme objected.

"No they won't!" Steven assured him. "It's up to us to persuade them."

"Yeah," Lucy agreed. "Mr Campbell will help us.

Remember when you first suggested doing up the lifeboat station, Steve? Dad would've just said no, but Mr Campbell listened."

"Well, if you think it's worth a try..." Graeme began.

"Definitely!" Alexander agreed. "We could even set up a web site to advertise our new visitors' centre, then persuade the whole village to go to the café and look it up!"

"Um, we wouldn't know how to—"

"Yes we would!" Graeme and Alexander chorused.

Bursting with confidence and enthusiasm, they agreed that Steven should try to persuade the grown-ups and Graeme would set up the web site.

"OK," Steven agreed. "I can do that! But we'll need to plan what to say first. Like, think about the problems before the grown-ups do."

"And find solutions before the grown-ups can!" Graeme said with satisfaction.

"Come on," said Lucy. "You can finish the woodwork lesson later. Let's go up to Hooper's Reach and make plans."

"Dad! Graeme's had this brilliant new idea!" Steven said, bursting into Reception with Graeme, Lucy and Alexander close behind him. His dad was writing up accounts with Bill Williamson, who had driven the laundry van to the site as long as Steven could remember. "We could have an Internet café in the village! Make a web site to advertise the new visitors' centre!"

"Computers!" Bill grumbled, scratching his bald head. "Never could get the hang of them!"

"But you could at the Internet café," Steven assured him. "There'd be people to help you."

"But Steven! Where are you going to get the computers from?" Dad said flatly.

"We've got it all worked out, Dad," Lucy said, joining in. "We could either ask four or five people to lend their computers for a week during the summer holidays, or maybe there's a company which would like to sponsor us."

"And where is this incredible project going to take place?" Dad asked, unconvinced.

"We thought we could ask to use a classroom at the primary school. And we'd ask someone to sell drinks and sweets and stuff, or make scones," Lucy explained.

"And wait 'till you hear the best bit, Dad!" Steven went on. "Graeme phoned his dad to tell him about it, and his dad said the law firm would give the money to have the phone lines put in!"

Steven's dad looked at Graeme, who grinned and nodded. Steven looked from Dad to Bill. "Hmm," Bill thought, scratching his chin. "At least that way, there'd be a greater net gain. If there was a firm involved, the village wouldn't have to pay so many overheads and extras. It'd be summer, so we wouldn't need heating..."

They were both silent for a moment, then Dad asked, "And who's going to be in charge of this project? I mean, do the teaching, and help all the people who are not very experienced with computers?"

"Well, Graeme can. He's fantastic with computers. And Alexander's quite good. And we thought of asking Mr Johnstone now he's retired.

He used to teach computing at the high school."

"Hmm. Jimmy Johnstone. He knows what he's talking about," Bill said thoughtfully. "He and I were at school together. He's told me several times that I ought to learn to use a computer. Window to the world, he calls it."

"Well, kids, I suppose you could put the idea to one or two of the village council members. Why not go and visit Mr Johnstone? You two could go together," he suggested, indicating Graeme and Steven. The phone rang, and Steven's dad said, "'Scuse me a minute," and picked up the receiver. "Hello, Anne-Marie. Yes, he's here. They're all here. Yes, all four of them." He paused, then he finished, "It's OK. No problem." Then he hung up. "Your mother, Alexander," he explained. "Checking where you are."

"Uh huh. Thanks, Mr MacGregor. I keep telling her not to worry, but she gets a bit uptight, you know, with the casino problems, an' all. Sorry."

"No problem, lad," Steven's dad assured him.

"Thanks, Dad. Bye, Bill," Steven said, and set off at a jog with the others following, leaving Bill scratching his head, and Dad shaking his.

On Friday morning, Steven was just finishing reading his Bible notes when he saw Mrs Granny walking up the path towards the cottage. He was glad to have an excuse to stop reading, because the passage was really difficult. Not difficult to understand. Just impossible to do. He had read from Luke chapter 6, verses 27 to 31. The quiz questions were easy:

'What should we do for our enemies?' he read.

'Love them,' he wrote.

'And for those who hate us?'

'Do good,' he wrote.

'And for those who curse us?'

'Bless them,' he wrote.

'And for those who are cruel to us?'

'Pray for them,' he wrote.

The next bit was worse: 'If anyone hits you on one cheek, let him hit the other one, too; if someone takes your coat, let him have your shirt as well.'

That's completely impossible, Steven thought, remembering how he and Alexander had fought when they first met, just because Alexander had insulted the Silver Cloud. God couldn't possibly mean it seriously. And what about Mr Curtis, and all the money problems he had?

The last verse for the day was the worst of all: 'Give to everyone who asks you for something, and when someone takes what is yours, do not ask for it back.'

So he stopped thinking about it, and instead he ran downstairs and opened the back door.

"Hello, dear!" Mrs Granny came in and sat down at the kitchen table. "What's this? Maths practice?" she asked, looking at Lucy's pink, yellow and green blocks. Mum looked up from the bills she was staring at, and put her calculator down.

"No," she explained. "It's Lucy's project countdown. It's like an advent calendar."

"My goodness! How organised she is!" Mrs Granny smiled. "Don't mind me, Jane," she added. "I really came to catch up with Steven."

"You're lucky to find him in," Mum replied.

"So I hear! Busy holiday, Steve?"

"You bet!" Steven said enthusiastically. "Alexander and I have built a new bird table so I could show him how to fix a 5 millimetre bit to the drill you gave him, and use screws instead of just hammer and nails. And we've taken out the Silver Cloud, and bought new sandals..." He stuck his feet out to show them off. Mum groaned.

"I can see you emptied the bank account there, Jane," Mrs Granny grinned.

"You're not kidding!" Mum replied. "I don't usually buy sports makes or designer labels. Ten pounds for the sandals and thirty for the name, I always say."

"But Mum, they're dead cool!" Steven objected. Time to change the subject, he thought, so he went on, "We've visited lots more people to check out the Internet café idea. Can you use a computer, Mrs Granny?"

"A bit. I can look up addresses and the site information that we've got stored. And I can type business letters on the word processor..."

"But how about the Internet?"

"Oh, I wouldn't have a clue about that. I'd love to try, though. That's what I came for. To ask how it's going. Have the council members agreed with your idea?"

"It looks like it," Steven said with satisfaction. "We went to ask Mr Johnstone what he thought, and he had a brilliant idea. He said we should ask if we could use the high school's computer suite. He's going to find out for us. And he says he'll help to teach anyone who wants to learn. And Mrs Curtis is going to do some baking and serve teas and things," Steven added. "There'll be sweets and fizzy drinks and stuff on sale all the time. It is meant to be a café, after all."

"Well, I think you've all done remarkably well," Mrs Granny beamed. "Especially you, Steven. You're the energy behind it all!"

Steven flushed with pleasure.

"Is Graeme going home soon?" Mrs Granny went on.

"Yes, tomorrow. It's school on Monday. We're going on a bike ride today to make the best of his last day."

"Where are you planning to go?"

"The old lifeboat station! We're going to take a camera so we can have photos of it now, then compare them when the whole thing's rebuilt!"

"You be careful now, love," Mum told him. "Take the lane. Don't go on the main road. And wear your helmet!"

"Mum!" Steven said, exasperated.

Chapter 7
Unwelcome visitors

"Bye Mum, I'm off," Steven called as he rode his bike out of the yard. He had his camera safely at the bottom of his rucksack, and two cans of cola and bags of crisps.

Mum appeared at the back door. "Bye love! Oh! You're not going to wear those sandals, are you? They're meant for the really hot weather."

"It is really hot, Mum!"

"Oh, all right. Be careful, then. Don't scrape them on that bike."

Steven sighed. "OK, Mum. Bye."

Graeme was already on his bike when Steven arrived at his caravan.

"Bye, Mrs Robertson. See you later!" Steven called, as they rode down to the bottom of the site and out on to the lane.

"Hey! Cool sandals!" Graeme said.

"Thanks," Steven replied. "We were going to get trainers, but they didn't have my size. These are a bit big, but I persuaded Mum I was going to grow over the summer!"

The sun was shining, and they got quite hot cycling. Steven had to stop to take his sweater off and stuff it into his rucksack.

When they reached the coast, the beach was deserted. "Bet it'll be full tomorrow," Steven observed. "It always is at the weekend if the sun shines."

"So this really will be a good place for a visitors' centre," Graeme observed.

"You bet," Steven agreed. "A brilliant place. Let's go to the old lifeboat station."

"D'you think we should walk?" Graeme suggested, looking at the pebbly path that led to the old building, about two hundred metres away. "The stones are very sharp. Might get punctures."

"Naw. Bikes are built for this sort of terrain," Steven replied confidently, pushing off towards the old station. Graeme followed more slowly, but they both arrived without damage to the bikes. They laid the bikes down at the back of the building, and walked slowly round it, talking about how much it was going to change, and inventing uses for each room. There were one or two old chairs lying around, and an old plastic table with metal legs. It was exciting to think how the place would be transformed.

Then they went down to the water's edge. The sea was very deep at the point where the slipway was submerged. They peered down into the black, murky depths, but they couldn't see anything. The sea was grey, despite the blue sky.

"Ugh! Looks freezing," Graeme observed. "Imagine capsizing in that!"

"Yeah! But plenty of people did. That's why the lifeboat station was built just here," Steven said. "I guess they still do get into trouble, but the Search and Rescue people pick them up instead." He picked up a stone the size of an egg, and hurled it as far as he could into the sea. It landed in the waves with a small splash.

"Bet I can beat that," Graeme claimed, picking up a similar sized stone.

"Bet you can't!" Steven laughed, accepting the challenge, and they threw stones until their arms ached.

"I'm going to take some photos," Steven announced, pulling his camera out of his rucksack.

"OK," said Graeme, running up to strike a pose leaning against the wall, and grinning like a toothpaste advert.

"Get lost!" Steven laughed, trying out various different angles. He took five shots of the building, each from a different place. Some had the cliffs in the background. Others had the sea.

"We should take some from the inside," Graeme suggested. "Then, when it's all repaired and painted, you'll be able to see what a change there's been."

"Yeah. All the doors are locked though," Steven said, checking.

"But the windows are so broken there must be one we can climb through."

So they walked slowly right round the building, checking for a window they could climb through without hurting themselves. Most of the windows were quite high, and they were just about to give up when Steven spotted a small window at the back where most of the glass had already been knocked out. "Look, if we break this last bit off, and prop my bike up against the wall, we could climb in and jump down."

It felt odd, breaking the last bit of glass out of the window. It made Steven feel like a vandal, even

punched another piece of glass out of the window. "'Ere, lads. Let's join 'em."

Steven's heart started to thud as the three boys scrambled through the window into the room. He told himself not to be scared. After all, he was supposed to be the brave boy who had spent all night in a shovel. The one with ideas. He looked at the boy who had thrown the rock. He was wearing a sleeveless T-shirt with a dragon design. Steven could see the muscles standing out on his arm as he climbed through the window, and a snake tattoo curling round his elbow.

"An' you!" No Hair pointed at Graeme. "You're the one what suggested the Internet café! You're the professor!" The three of them started to bow and scrape in front of Graeme with sneering mock admiration. "Brilliant idea, Your Brainship!"

Come on, Graeme, Steven thought, you're the intelligent one. Think of something stunning to say! But Graeme remained silent.

"Very clever, Sir Swotbags!" Lanky agreed.

"Naw! He was right, lads," the Shot Put said, stopping them. "It is a good idea. I'll use the Internet café. My ol' man never lets me on the net for very long. Says it costs too much. And anyway, he always wants to check on what sites I look up! Says they might not be suitable. Know what I mean?" He sniggered, and the others joined in.

Lanky picked up Steven's rucksack. "What you got in 'ere then, Scrawny?" He tipped the bag upside down. Steven wanted to stop him, but his knees had suddenly turned to jelly. His sweatshirt and the cans of cola and crisps fell into the dust and splinters of glass. "Oh! Grub! 'Ow kind. Pity you didn't bring three, though, eh?" Lanky tossed a bag of crisps to No Hair, and a can to the Shot Put, then opened the other can and took a long swig.

"Hey, those are ours!" Graeme objected, lunging at Lanky and making a grab for the can.

"Now, steady on, Prof. Don't be greedy," said the Shot Put, grabbing one of Graeme's arms and pinning it behind him, forcing him to his knees.

"Wanted some juice, eh?" said Lanky. "'Ere y'are then." And he poured the rest of the cola over Graeme's head, so it ran down his hair and face and soaked his sweater. Anger tussled with fear inside Steven. It made the blood race round his body, but it seemed to glue him to the spot.

No reason to be scared, he told himself. They're only boys.

They're big and mean, he answered himself back. And there are three of them. When a cat catches a mouse, it just plays with it until it gets bored. Then it pounces.

The Shot Put released Graeme, who stood up and wiped his face with his sleeve. Opening the second can, the strong boy took a long drink, then handed it to No Hair, and burped loudly. No Hair finished the can and threw it through the window.

"Got anything else, Scrawny?" Lanky asked, shaking the rucksack and feeling in the pocket. Steven felt his throat tighten. His heart was hammering so hard, he thought the boys might hear it.

Holding his breath, he prayed silently, Lord, don't let them find the camera or the bikes.

"What you in 'ere for then?" No Hair looked hard at Steven.

Feeling himself reddening, Steven replied, "Just looking round, like you."

Please, Lord, please, he prayed, his hands clenched, and his nails digging into his palms.

"Wondering if it's worth it, eh?" Lanky asked. "Rebuild this place, an' it'll end up the same again in a few years, you'll see."

"It won't!" Graeme declared, his fists clenched. "It'll be..."

"Oh, don't you worry your clever little head, Prof. You'll get your reward. There'll be a bronze plaque by the front door – 'Prof and Scrawny rebuilt this heap'. And the date. But we can leave our mark now!" He pulled a can of red spray paint from his pocket and scrawled on the wall 'SB and PR and CH woz ere'. Then he added some drops, which looked like blood. He stood back to admire his work.

Please, Lord, please, Steven prayed. With a huge effort of self-control, he managed not to glance towards the kitchen or the back window where they had climbed in. He didn't want to give the boys ideas.

"C'mon, lads, this is borin'," said No Hair, and he turned and vaulted lightly through the broken window.

"Tell you what though, Prof," the Shot Put said to Graeme as he followed No Hair out of the window. "Why don't you make this place into an Internet café? That'd be more interesting than a museum of birds' feathers."

"See ya, Scrawny," said Lanky, as he scrambled through the window. Steven let his breath out slowly, and felt his heart slow down.

The Shot Put kicked the can that No Hair had thrown out of the window, and the three of them made a triangle, dribbling and passing the can between them. After a moment or two, the Shot Put got bored with the game, and gave a half-hearted kick. "What was that?" Lanky complained. "Give it some welly!" So the Shot Put aimed an energetic kick that sent his trainer flying off his foot and into the sea with an agonising splash.

The three boys stared, speechless for a moment. Then the Shot Put yelled, "That was your fault, Stew!"

"How was it my fault?" Lanky complained angrily.

"You told me to kick it harder."

"Quit complaining, Henderson, and get in there and get it!" No Hair told him. So, as Steven and Graeme watched from the broken window, the Shot Put stood at the edge of the water, took off his other trainer and his socks and prepared to wade in. The lost trainer floated temptingly ten metres from the rocks, then began slowly to fill with water and sink. The Shot Put rolled up the legs of his jeans and stepped nervously into the water.

"It's freezing!" he gasped.

"Don't be such a wimp!" Lanky challenged him. He and No Hair moved to stand next to him at the water's edge.

Steven knew that the submerged rocks were sharp and slippery, and the water became instantly deep. The coastline was famously dangerous, and even strong swimmers could die within minutes because of the cold. A jumble of ideas flashed through his mind. He remembered his Bible reading: 'Love your enemies. Bless those who curse you. Do good to those who hate you. Pray for those who are cruel to you.'

Lord, please look after him, Steven pleaded silently. Please help him.

Then he whispered urgently to Graeme, "Come on, let's climb out."

"No," Graeme said. "They've forgotten about us. If they remember, they'll make us go into the water to fetch it." But Steven was already half way out, balancing carefully, trying to avoid cutting himself. He jumped down on the outside, and Graeme followed.

"Don't go in," Steven suddenly told the Shot Put. "It's too dangerous."

The Shot Put looked at him, surprised, then he seemed to agree with him because he stepped out again on to the dry rock. He put his socks and one trainer back on, then he looked around at the stony pathway. "You'll have to give me a piggy back, Stew," he said, jumping on to Lanky's back. Lanky staggered a few paces, then dumped the Shot Put on to the stones.

"No way, Henderson. You're an elephant."

"Ow!" the Shot Put complained, sitting down and holding his socked foot.

'If someone takes your coat, let him have your shirt as well!' The morning's Bible reading rang through Steven's head.

"You can have my sandals!" Steven said suddenly, taking them off and throwing them to the Shot Put. He felt so grateful that they hadn't taken or damaged his camera or the bikes. And he reckoned he could ride his bike home in his socks, without putting his feet down.

The three boys stared at him in amazed silence for a moment, then the Shot Put said, "Why?"

"Er, well, because I've got, er, I've got, er..." He still didn't want to mention the bikes.

"Never mind him," No Hair told the Shot Put. "That's his look out."

"Steve!" Graeme hissed.

"Hey, cool sandals!" Lanky murmured, squatting down beside the Shot Put. Taking his one trainer off, the stocky boy tried on the sandals, glancing suspiciously at Steven all the time. His feet were broad but short, and although the sandals were a couple of sizes too small, it didn't matter because the toes and heels were open and he could adjust the straps.

"Steven!" Graeme whispered again, tugging at Steven's sleeve. "Your mum'll go crazy..."

"Hey, Scrawny?" said No Hair. "Know what?" Steven said nothing. "You're a nut case. That's what!" And he roared with laughter, and the three of them walked away down the stony path, back towards the village.

Chapter 8
Twenty-four seven

It was a few moments before Graeme spoke. Then he exploded, "What did you do that for? Your mum said to be careful with the new sandals. You were proud of them. You said so. Those boys are just scum. You didn't have to do anything for them." Steven looked at Graeme now. He was scowling, and his face was white with anger. "They were right," Graeme added. "You *are* a nut case."

Steven took a breath to explain, but he let it out again. What would he say? That he was nervous about the Shot Put getting into difficulties in the water? Or would he try to explain that he had read a bit in the Bible which said you should give more than you were asked? He so desperately wanted Graeme to become a Christian, but he always seemed to make a mess of helping him to understand.

Graeme was right about Mum. She'd be hopping mad. Maybe he *was* a nut case. Maybe Graeme was right about that, too.

He sighed, and said, "We've got bikes. At least I can ride home without having to walk on the stones. At least they didn't find the bikes."

Graeme didn't answer. Instead, he picked up a large stone and hurled it at one of the windows, smashing the glass that was left and sending it skittering across the floor and broken furniture. Then he stomped round to the back of the building.

Picking his way carefully back to the window which the boys had smashed, Steven climbed in again, retrieved his camera gratefully, picked up his rucksack, and then hoisted himself out at the back where the bikes were. He and Graeme set off back to the caravan site without speaking. Graeme rode in front, his shoulders hunched, his sweatshirt stained and his hair sticky with cola. Steven rode behind him, trying not to put a foot down.

They didn't pass the three boys. Perhaps they had caught a bus, Steven thought, relieved. But as he rode on in silence, a strange, light feeling seemed to fill him. He had succeeded! He had read in his Bible that you should be willing to give more than people asked you for. And he had! He had obeyed one of God's most difficult instructions. Suddenly he felt happy. Even though he had no idea how he was going to explain to Mum and Dad. He felt himself grinning like an idiot. Back at the site, they rode through the gate into Steven's back yard. Graeme rode on, back to his caravan, muttering something that Steven couldn't catch, and not meeting his eye.

"Graeme!" Steven called. "Hang on a minute!" But Graeme ignored him. Putting his bike away in the shed, Steven went to the back door of the cottage with his heart thudding. Whatever was his mum going to say? He tried the door. It was locked. Of course! He and Graeme were back earlier than they had planned. Mum and Dad must be in Reception, or round the site somewhere. Steven breathed a sigh of relief. It gave him time to think.

He picked up the back door key from its hiding place behind the plant pot, and went in and up to his room. He put on his old trainers, then stood at his window, looking up to Hooper's Reach.

Thank you, Lord, he whispered. Thank you for helping me. And thank you for not letting the boys find the camera or the bikes. And thank you for... for... he didn't know why he felt so happy.

Still grinning, he turned to sit on his bed and try to think out what to tell Mum. Ideas of making up tall stories flitted through his mind. Porkies. Fibs. The boys had stolen the sandals. He had left them by the sea to go for a paddle, and they'd disappeared. Or he could just hope Mum would forget about the sandals, and nothing would ever be said, until he grew so tall, and he could say he'd grown out of them long ago.

Lies. Steven knew them for what they were, and he wouldn't insult his mum by telling them. Mrs Granny always said that going to church was only a part of being a Christian. You had to be a 24/7 Christian. Twenty-four hours a day, seven days a week. He'd tell Mum he wanted to be a Christian all the time. Then he'd tell Graeme, too...

The back door opened, and Steven heard Mum and Lucy come in, chattering. Someone else was with them, too. "Hello!" It was Mum's voice. "Steve?"

Please help me, Lord, Steven prayed, running down the stairs.

"Hi, Mum! I—" He stopped and stared. He stared at what she was holding.

"Steve!" she said, annoyed. "I told you to look after your new sandals. What did you leave them in the yard for?" She held up his sandals, the heel straps dangling, undone.

"Oh!" he gasped. "Oh, I—"

"Put them in your room, and come down and help Lucy and Amanda and me to make Goliath's armour," Mum said, putting the sandals down on the stairs. She went into the kitchen, and Steven stood still in astonishment. God had answered his prayer before he'd even prayed it! The Shot Put must have known where he lived. Everyone in the village seemed to know since the incident with the JCB. He must have thrown them into the yard. He can't have been complete scum after all.

Picking up the sandals, Steven put them away in his wardrobe, then went downstairs. Amanda was asking about the countdown blocks. "Fifty-seven days until the parade then? That's ages!"

"Best to get started with what we can, as early as we can," Mum advised. "New ideas keep popping up all the time!"

Steven interrupted to tell Mum and the girls about the photos he'd taken of the old lifeboat station before the renovations began, so they'd be able to compare them later. He didn't tell them about the three boys. Not 'till he'd had time to think. Neither did he tell them about the idea that had been niggling at the back of his mind all afternoon, despite everything else that had happened. An Internet café at the new visitors' centre! It was the Shot Put's idea. He hadn't been serious, but Steven was, now, as he thought about it. But it was much too soon to tell Mum or Dad. The only person he wanted to tell was Graeme. But he wasn't sure whether Graeme was even speaking to him just now.

Lucy had a bin bag full of empty cereal packets. She and Amanda set to work with pencils and rulers and began measuring five centimetre strips. "Here, Steve, can you cut these out?" Lucy asked, handing him a pair of scissors.

Cutting out strips of card was not normally Steven's scene, but today he felt unusually upbeat. "OK," he grinned. "What are they for?"

"Mum's going to stick on silver foil, and attach them to a belt, like so," she demonstrated, holding them up to her waist, "and more pieces for the shoulders, and they're going to be Goliath's armour. Do them pointed at the end, Steve, like this." She took the scissors from him and made two cuts, so that one end of the first strip was pointed.

"OK," he grinned cheerfully, not minding her bossiness.

Amanda looked up at him and smiled. Then she turned to his mum. "Mrs MacGregor?"

"Mmm?"

"What is Mr MacGregor going to wear to drive the Holiday Club float?"

"Wait and see!" said Mum, mysteriously.

"Mum!" Steven and Lucy said together. It was the first Steven had heard of it. He just couldn't imagine his dad dressing up at all.

Lucy and Amanda drew and cut, chatted and laughed, and Steven's happiness lasted throughout the afternoon. He felt better than he would have believed possible after the frightening encounter with the boys and an argument with his best friend.

Then he had a brainwave. "Mum?" he asked suddenly. "Can I ask Mr Johnstone to help me set up an e-mail address on the computer in Reception?"

"E-mail? You?"

"Yes! Then I can write to Graeme after he gets home."

On Monday evening Mr Johnstone called at the cottage to give Steven a lesson. "Now, which is your ISP?" he asked Steven, as Mum went to fetch the key to Reception.

"Er..."

"Your Internet Service Provider?" Mr Johnstone translated.

"Um, I don't know," Steven admitted. "Better ask Mum." He hated to show his ignorance.

Mr Johnstone seemed to understand. "We'll soon solve that problem," he said cheerfully. He chatted with Mum for a few minutes using words which Steven could only guess at.

While he was waiting for them, Steven leafed through the newspaper. A headline caught his attention:

'Greedy for Gain; cheating the cheats'.

Steven read on: 'Gambling club owners organise a network to track down cheats. But who's cheating who?' The article continued about a man who woke up in the middle of the night to find his house surrounded by thugs who threatened him if he didn't pay up. Steven shuddered and thought of the Curtises.

"OK, Steven, I'm all ready. Let's go," Mr Johnstone said, and Steven didn't have time to finish the article or to worry about it for very long as they set off across the site towards Reception.

"I've had a word with the head teacher and the education authority about using the school's computer suite," Mr Johnstone told him, "and it looks like we're on! They said it seemed like an excellent idea for the village. A couple of my former colleagues have agreed to help out, too. The computers are all set up; the drinks and snacks can be served in the classroom next door, so all we'd have to pay out would be rent to the education authority. All the rest of the income would go to the project. It would all be net gain."

"Net gain," Steven repeated. "Graeme said that. So did Mr Williamson. What does it mean?"

"The net gain is the amount of profit you make. It's what you have left when you've paid all your expenses."

Steven started to giggle.

"What's so funny?"

"Net gain. Internet! Get it?" Mr Johnstone groaned.

"Sandy Campbell was suggesting the café should run for the last two weeks of July," Mr Johnstone went on.

"Starting before the parade?"

"Yes. One week before and one week after."

"Mr Campbell must be so busy!" Steven reflected.

"Yes, he is. His wife says she never sees him! But he's very organised. And he's got mates to help him. Do you know Ronnie Fergusson?" Steven shook his head. "He's a police dog handler. He's going on the police float with Sandy and half a dozen others. They're going to head up the parade."

"Wow! It's really happening!" Steven exclaimed. "It's seemed ages to wait, but now it's only twenty-six days to go 'till the opening of the café!"

"What are you? A walking calculator?" Mr Johnstone laughed.

Steven grinned and explained Lucy's countdown blocks.

"Hmm. What a very orderly young lady your sister must be!"

In Reception, Steven pulled up a second chair in front of the computer monitor, and Mr Johnstone switched it on. "Now, see these little pictures down the left-hand side?" Steven nodded. "They're called icons. See this one?" He pointed. "Move the mouse, that's right, and double click on that icon. See that box?" He pointed again. "That's to set up an address for a new user. That's you. Now, you have to choose a name. Your own name's too long, and anyway, there are probably other Steven MacGregors. Do you have a nickname?"

Steven thought for a moment. "No, not really. But how about Hooper? After Hooper's Reach?"

"Sounds OK. And to make it unique, just your own, you should include a number. Your house number, or your birthday, or something like that."

"Er, how about 630?"

"OK. Is that a special number?"

"Yes," Steven said. It was the chapter and verse of the Bible reading in Luke that he had put into practice. But he didn't want to explain that to Mr Johnstone just then.

"Right. So type in hooper630 just here." He pointed to a box on the screen. "And you need a secret password. You can type it in just here while I'm not looking." He stabbed his finger at the screen. "But type carefully with no mistakes because on the screen you'll only see asterisks.

Don't bother with capital letters, and don't leave any gaps."

Steven puzzled for a moment, then he wrote in 'netgain'. He typed carefully with one finger, searching for each letter.

The process was slow, but Mr Johnstone was patient and he explained everything one step at a time. By the end of the evening, Steven knew how to type in Graeme's e-mail address, choose a subject, write the message, place it in the outbox and click 'send and receive'.

"hello" he wrote, "guess what i ve got an email address write back steve"

Then Mr Johnstone went over it several times so Steven wouldn't forget. They closed down the computer, locked up the Reception chalet and walked back towards the cottage.

"Thanks very much," Steven said as Mr Johnstone cut across the grass to go back to his car. Steven stood to wave him off, then he jogged back to Reception. Unlocking the door and switching the computer on again, he double clicked on the ISP icon and wrote another message to Graeme:

"very sorry about the row get a bible look up luke ch 6 v 27 to 31 i was trying to do it"

Feeling nervous, hopeful and very pleased with himself, he jogged home and tried to wait patiently for Graeme to reply.

"It's easy, Mum!" Steven declared, as he burst through the cottage door on Tuesday evening. He found Mrs Curtis in the kitchen, talking with Mum and Lucy.

"Oh, er, hello Mrs Curtis."

"Hi, honey."

"Steve, look!" Lucy said, delighted. "Mrs Curtis has bought me a blue countdown block from Mitchell's. So the blue one is for the café. It's only twenty-five days to go."

"No problem!" Steven declared. "We'll be ready. We can do it!"

"What's easy, love?" Mum asked finally.

"Sending and receiving e-mails! Mr Johnstone showed me how yesterday, and today I got an e-mail back from Graeme." He was thrilled at his own success, but even more thrilled that Graeme had replied so promptly.

"Mum," he added thoughtfully.

"What, love?"

"Mr Johnstone said you could have taught me any time. He said you're as good on the computer as he is."

"He's flattering me, son. He's brilliant!"

"But why haven't you told me how to set up an e-mail address, Mum?"

"Because you've never shown any interest in it before, love. If anything requires you to sit down for more than five minutes, you start fidgeting!"

Steven grinned. He had to admit it was true. But he was changing now. Somehow it was easier to sort out the argument with Graeme on e-mail than it was face-to-face. At least Graeme couldn't see him blushing! He went up to his room to read the two e-mails. He had learned how to print them off.

"I see your point," Graeme had written back. "I'd never thought about it before. Being a Christian is really different! Great news about the café. See you in July. We're hoping to make it for the talent contest. G."

"PS Mum's going to enter for the half-marathon! She's training every day!"

Chapter 9

Craft and talent

By the time June began the village was buzzing with activity. Every evening and weekend people came jogging down the lane, preparing for the half-marathon. Dad had agreed to sponsor several people to finish the course. Mrs Granny had knitted a sweater with a beautiful Shetland design, and Mrs Curtis had made a patchwork cot quilt for the craft competition. Two girls from the high school had been to the caravan site every Saturday to wash cars for a fee. Sandy Campbell organised a car treasure hunt, which had everyone driving around the countryside looking for clues.

With just thirteen days to go until the craft competition and talent contest, Steven's bird box was nearly finished. Lucy had wanted to make a new wildlife book for her entry, but everyone had persuaded her to enter the original book, the one Steven had used for information for his speech in the JCB shovel. Everyone agreed it was already perfect. Her writing was neat and the drawings were beautiful. Exquisite, Mrs Curtis had said. Cool, Alexander had agreed.

The day of the craft competition and talent contest finally arrived. Crafts of every description decked the tables, which had been rigged up around the edge of the village hall. There were embroidered tablecloths and cushion covers, cross-stitched pictures, knitted sweaters, soft toys, pots, sculptures, paintings, models, flower arrangements, Steven's nesting box, Graeme's computer-printed poster sent in advance, Lucy's wildlife scrapbook and Amanda's aunty Carrie's handmade jewellery.

As they walked around the exhibits, Steven kept looking towards the doorway, wondering if Graeme would arrive.

"Hello Anne-Marie!" It was Mrs Mitchell from the newsagents. "How are you? And how are the plans for the Internet café? I hear you're organising the catering."

Mrs Curtis laughed. "Well, the real organiser is young Steven, here, and his buddy Graeme. I think I've got the easy job. We're using the same Cash and Carry firm that Rhoda uses for the caravan site, and we've put in a big order for cans and cartons of juice, crisps and chocolate bars. All the usual popular stuff. And there's going to be some home-baking too, of course."

"Put me down for three dozen tray bakes!" Mrs Mitchell offered cheerfully. "We'll be along during the week. I'm looking forward to brushing up my skills, and maybe learning some new ones."

When they had moved on, Steven whispered to Alexander, "Do you think people will really come? To the café, I mean. What if everyone works so hard for it, and nobody comes?"

"Gee, I dunno, Steve. I hadn't thought about that. Tell you what…"

"What?"

"Remember those fliers Graeme did last Easter about signing the petition for Hooper's Reach?"

"Yeah?"

"Why don't we make some fliers like that advertising the café, and distribute them round the caravan site and the village?"

"Yeah!" Steven exclaimed, perking up. "We'll have to be quick, though. It's not long 'til the opening ceremony. If Graeme does come today, we could start this evening!"

At two o'clock Mr Johnstone, the compère for the afternoon, rapped on the table on the platform and asked everyone to take a seat. "Lucy!" Steven hissed. "Save those two seats on the end in case Graeme and his mum come."

Mr Johnstone introduced the celebrity for the afternoon, the mayor of the Old Town, who announced the prize winners previously agreed upon by the village council. Steven didn't win a prize. Neither did Lucy or Graeme. But Steven was pleased to learn that the winner was Amanda's aunty Carrie. Using the semi-precious gemstones she had found locally, along with hand-beaten silver, she had produced pretty, delicate earrings, brooches, pendants, bracelets and cuff links. She certainly deserved a prize.

With the minimum rearrangement on the stage, and a little shuffling among the audience, the talent contest got underway. Sitting together on the second row of seats, Steven, Lucy and Alexander had an excellent view. Mrs MacKenzie told funny stories that made everyone roar with laughter. Sandy Campbell did life-like impersonations of politicians and television personalities. Bill Williamson, the laundry van driver, played a Spanish Flamenco guitar piece, and everyone gasped at the fact that he had been hiding his talent for so long.

Steven enjoyed all the entries, but he was planning to give his vote to Amanda, who had sung 'A Perfect Day' with a backing tape. She was dressed up in black velvet trousers with a sparkly silver top, which made her look much older. And her voice was fantastic. She could hold a note and look at the audience, and she didn't seem shy at all.

Just before the last entry, there was a small commotion at the back of the hall. Everyone turned round, and Graeme and his mother crept in, apologising for interrupting.

"How's it going?" Graeme whispered.

"Cool!" Steven replied. "You should have heard Amanda."

"The last contestant, ladies and gentleman, is not unknown to us," said Mr Johnstone. "In fact, it's our own village minister, the Reverend MacKenzie."

Everyone clapped and Mr MacKenzie stepped on to the stage. There was an excited rustle of anticipation among the smaller Holiday Club children on the front row. Mr Johnstone helped him to lift a small round table into the centre of the stage. It had a floor-length red tablecloth, and on top was Mr MacKenzie's sparkling magician's suitcase. He grinned at the audience, and opened the case so that only he could see into it.

"Is there any magic in the air today, children?" he asked them.

"Yes!" shouted Mr Johnstone's grandson, Chris, from the front row.

"I think you're right!" Mr MacKenzie exclaimed, coming down from the stage to pull a small silk square from behind Chris's ear. He caught a couple more from the top of Lucy's head and one from underneath Steven's chair. The children gasped with amazement, and everyone clapped. Then he threw a sponge ball to Graeme. "Just hold on to that for me, son, while I get ready here." He returned to the stage and rummaged in his case. "Now don't let go of it," he told Graeme. "Just squeeze it in your hand."

He brought a jug out of his suitcase. It was filled with water. He produced several glasses. "Now," he muttered, "what did I do with those three balls?" He looked around until his eyes rested on Graeme. "Ah, you, son. I gave the three balls to you, didn't I?"

"No, only one," Graeme replied.

"Only one? You must have made a mistake. I've lost three, you see. Let's check. Come up here, son."

Still clasping his hand closed, Graeme went up on to the stage. "Now, open your palm slowly," Mr MacKenzie told him. There, in Graeme's palm, were three small sponge balls. Graeme gasped, and so did the audience. "Got a short memory, lad, that's your trouble," Mr MacKenzie joked, and the audience laughed and clapped again.

Graeme sat down grinning, and Mr MacKenzie went on, "I haven't got any special powers. But God has. Just watch what he can do. Now, who'd like a drink of water?" No one responded. "It's OK," Mr MacKenzie chuckled. "It's not poisoned or anything!" He poured some water from the jug into one of the glasses, and drank it down. "Ah! Very refreshing. Now, anyone?"

Amanda offered, and went up on to the stage. Pouring some water into another glass for her, Mr MacKenzie invited others. Amanda drank her water, and agreed that it was very refreshing. "Have you noticed," Mr MacKenzie asked them, "the water never runs out?" He poured some for several other children who came eagerly for a glass of water. "Like God's love, it never runs out! There's always enough for everyone!" He poured as he talked, and handed out glasses to the children. Steven didn't take his eyes off the jug. It was true. No matter how much water Mr MacKenzie poured, there always seemed to be more. "Now, off you go," he said, shooing the children off the stage, "If you drink any more, you'll need the toilet before I get to the end of the show!" They ran back to their seats, giggling.

"You know, ladies and gentlemen, boys and girls, I sometimes hear people say they're bored. The older ones say their jobs are boring. The children complain they've nothing to do. But I'll tell you what I've discovered." He delved into his suitcase, and brought out a child's colouring book. "If you don't have Jesus as your friend, it can be a bit dull. Like this." He held the colouring book out to the audience and flicked through the pages. "Nothing but black and white. Colourless." Steven looked at the outlines of buckets and spades, toy trucks, clowns and beach balls. He remembered having a colouring book just like it.

"When I was much younger," Mr MacKenzie told them, closing the book for a moment, "I didn't know Jesus. Well, I knew a bit about him, but I didn't know him as a real friend. And I used to get bored. And, of course, then I used to get into trouble. Then one day someone told me that Jesus is alive today, and that he has good plans for my life. I said 'OK, Lord. Whatever you say'. He became my friend, and life has never been boring since."

Holding the book out to the audience, Mr MacKenzie flicked through it again. This time, all the pictures were beautifully coloured in! The beach ball was red and yellow. A green bucket lay on the golden sand beside a blue sea. Steven couldn't believe it. The smaller children on the front row had begun to stand up to get a better view. Steven stole a glance at Graeme. His eyes were wide. "Wow!" He whispered in Steven's ear. "How did he do that?"

Steven enjoyed the trick as much as everyone, but what Mr MacKenzie had said was good, too. It was true, he reflected. Ever since he'd been sure that Jesus was his friend, life had been full of surprises.

"Another thing God can do," Mr MacKenzie was continuing, "is that he can put broken lives back together." Rummaging in his suitcase again, he produced a skipping rope. "Who's good at skipping?" Lucy's hand shot up. "Come up here, young lady," Mr MacKenzie invited her.

Lucy stepped on to the stage, and Mr MacKenzie asked her to check the skipping rope. "No knots?" Lucy shook her head. "No torn bits?" Lucy shook her head again. "Have a go with it, Lucy. Show us that it's a good rope, and you're a good skipper."

Lucy turned the rope forward a few times, then backwards. Then she crossed and uncrossed her arms. "Showing off," Steven grumbled to Alexander.

"It's a good strong rope, ladies and gentlemen," Mr MacKenzie observed, taking it from Lucy. "But sometimes bad things happen to ropes, just as disasters can happen to lives." He took a big pair of scissors from his suitcase, grasped the rope in the middle, and cut it!

"Oh," Lucy exclaimed.

"Don't worry, Lucy," Mr MacKenzie smiled. "Just when it looks like everything's hopeless, God can step in." Taking hold of the rope, he ran a hand down smoothly from one end to the other, and it became one long, strong, continuous rope. The audience gasped, cheered, whistled and shouted. Mr MacKenzie gave the rope back to Lucy, and asked her to skip again. She did so, but this time she gave it back after a few turns and didn't show off.

"Amazing, ladies and gentlemen? Yes! But it's even more amazing how God can put damaged lives back together again." Lucy returned to her seat, and as he leaned to let her push past, Steven noticed Alexander. He was staring, unblinking, at Mr MacKenzie, and his blue eyes shone with hope in his pale face. For the first time, Steven wondered what it must be like when your dad is thousands of miles away, and you've no idea when you're going to see him again, nor what's going to happen. Lord, he prayed silently, Please put the Curtises' lives back together again.

No one was surprised when Mr MacKenzie was declared the winner, and everyone was delighted when he presented his prize to Amanda. "A meal for four in the pizza restaurant in the Old Town. Take your mum and a couple of friends," he said. Steven hoped he might be one of the friends.

The following afternoon, Graeme, Lucy and Steven designed and printed enough fliers advertising the café for everyone on the caravan site, and most homes in the village.

"Only twelve days to go!" Lucy exclaimed, tearing off a paper from the blue block.

"Well, twelve days is just about right for advertising," Mum commented. "Enough to give people warning, but not enough for them to forget all about it."

So the four children, with Mrs Curtis, Mrs Robertson and Steven's mum and dad taking it in turns, spent a couple of hours each afternoon tramping round the village, delivering leaflets. Graeme printed an extra large one that Mrs Mitchell stuck in the window of the newsagent's.

There were only seven days to go to the opening of the café, fourteen to the parade and twenty-one to the marathon and prize giving. Dad made a mysterious trip into Glasgow, and refused to tell anyone why. Steven and Lucy were forbidden to look inside his wardrobe. "All will be revealed!" was all he would say.

Chapter 10
Coffee and surfing

"Steve! Lucy! Hurry up!" Mum called up the stairs. "Important day today!"

Steven looked at his clock. Eight o'clock. It was two hours before the Internet café opened.

"In a minute, Mum," Lucy called down the stairs. "I'm just finishing something."

"Do it later, pet. Come now," Mum called.

"Why the rush?" Lucy asked Steven as they went downstairs and sat at the table. Pouring cereal into a bowl, Steven asked, "Mind if I change the radio station, Mum?" It was tuned into local radio, and he preferred a music station.

"Not yet, love. I just want to listen to what's coming up next."

So Steven and Lucy sat and munched their breakfast, and Steven listened with half an ear while the announcer warned of road works on the A9 and an accident blocking one of the lanes of the M8.

Then the announcer said, "And now for Action West! At a loose end on this drizzly Saturday morning? Get out and about in the west! There's a lot to do today. And top of the list is a new venture. Calling all computer-lovers around the vicinity of the Old King's High School. There's a new community Internet café opening at ten o'clock this morning. It's being organised by a couple of enterprising local youngsters who want to raise money to renovate the old lifeboat station off Westerley Point. Graeme Robertson and Steven MacGregor have put a lot of time and effort into this idea with the help of their friend, Alexander Curtis, Steven's sister, Lucy, and their teacher, Mr Jimmy Johnstone. So get out there and support them! There'll be a café with drinks and goodies, and plenty of techno-help if you're a novice with a PC. Well done, lads! Hope it goes well for you today!"

Steven and Lucy looked at each other. Lucy was poised with her spoon halfway to her mouth. Steven looked at Mum. She was grinning from ear to ear.

"Mum! You knew! You knew he was going to say that! How did you know?"

"Sandy Campbell told me he'd phoned an advert into the local station," she explained. "He said they usually put them on at around eight. I didn't want you to miss it!"

"Oh, wow!" Lucy exclaimed, dropping her spoon into her milk with a splash. "We were on the radio!"

"We're famous!" Steven said, standing up and punching the air. "Wonder if Graeme heard it?"

"I think he might have because I tipped off Mrs Robertson. Told her to switch on the radio in the caravan at about eight o'clock."

"D'you think lots of people will come?" Lucy asked.

"I sincerely hope so," Mum said, "after all the advertising we've done. And the weather's on our side. It's too wet for the beach today, but the rain's not hard enough to stop people getting out."

"They said Mr Johnstone was your teacher," Lucy observed.

"Pity he won't be at the high school when I start there," Steven complained. "I bet he was a brilliant teacher."

"Come on, you two. Wash up your bowls and let's get going. And change into your trainers, Steven. Your feet'll get soaked in those sandals today."

"The trainers are getting a bit small for me, Mum. They rub my toes."

"Oh, OK," Mum sighed, and she didn't insist.

An enthusiastic crowd had gathered outside the high school by the time Steven arrived with Mum, Lucy and Alexander. Graeme was already there, helping to set up the computers with Mr Johnstone and two of the teachers who lived in the village. Mrs Granny and Mrs Curtis had also arrived early to prepare the snacks.

In the excited buzz of conversation Steven overheard all sorts of different comments.

"Hope there's someone there to teach us. I don't have a clue."

"My dad never lets me look up football team sites at home. He's always on the net himself."

"I'm going to send e-mails to all my friends in America."

"There'd better be some good food. I'm starving."

As soon as Mr Johnstone invited people in, there was an excited rush to have a look around and check out the place. Some people sat down immediately at the computers and their fingers whizzed over the keys with confidence. Mrs Granny was busy immediately serving coffee to people who just came to look round, while Graeme hovered around politely, ready to help an older man who was eager to have a go at using the computer for the first time.

"I'm going to look up organisations that help endangered species," Lucy announced. "Come and help me, Alexander."

"What do you want to do, love?" Mum asked Steven. "Want a drink while you're thinking about it?"

Steven looked around. There must have been twenty computers, and most of them were now occupied. Some people sat in twos, moving a chair to sit next to a friend, then peering at the screen together. The adjoining room was usually a classroom, but Mrs Granny and Mrs Curtis had transformed it into a colourful café with bright tablecloths, menus, posters and a range of delicious snacks. Just across the corridor was a small room with a kettle, fridge and sink for washing up cups and glasses. It looked quite different from the way Steven remembered it from his introductory trip round the school with his primary class.

Mum put a glass of orange juice in front of him. "Do you want to have a look on the net? Or write an e-mail? Or just watch?" she asked him.

Steven didn't know what he wanted to do. After all the excitement, he could hardly believe it was actually happening. But he sipped his orange juice slowly and took in all the activity. There had been so much planning, advertising and ordering of food and supplies. Sandy Campbell had put an advert in the local newspaper, and Mrs Curtis had drawn up a rota of helpers. And all the time, Steven had wondered if it would all work. What if nobody came? What if they all had computers at home already? What if people thought it wasn't really what the village wanted?

But as he watched everyone chatting, laughing, eating and drinking, staring at screens and tapping away on the keyboards, he felt a tremendous satisfaction. It was working. It was a success. He breathed out and stretched.

"Happy, love?" Mum asked.

"You bet!" he grinned.

"Colin Henderson!" It was Mrs Granny's voice. "How nice to see you again, dear. How are you?" Steven turned round to look, and there at the counter, ordering a lemonade, was the Shot Put! Without thinking, Steven looked down at his feet. He was wearing newish trainers.

"Fine, thanks, Mrs G," the Shot Put replied.

"Are you still at school, dear, or..."

"Just left. Looking for a college place. Want to be a carpenter and joiner," the Shot Put replied. "Came to look up college courses on the net. Need a part-time job, too. My ol' man says I gotta bring in some money." He pulled a face.

"Carpenter and joiner, eh?" said Mrs Granny thoughtfully. "I'll keep my eyes and ears open."

Glancing round the room to look for a seat, the Shot Put spotted Steven. Their eyes met for a moment, then the Shot Put looked down at Steven's feet. Steven noticed the ghost of a smile playing around his mouth. Then he turned away, and Steven went up to the counter. "Who's that boy, Mrs Granny?" he whispered.

"Who? Oh, that's Colin Henderson. Used to be in my Sunday school class a long time ago. Had a lot of problems. Used to throw his weight around, but I've heard he's calmed down a bit recently. I never give up praying for any of them."

"Any of who?"

"Any of the youngsters who were in my class at one time or another. Who knows what fine plans God has for them all?"

Steven bought a packet of crisps and went over to watch Alexander and Lucy. "Say, d'ya know what'd be neat?" Alexander asked suddenly. "We could have a chat. Live e-mail. Use instant messaging." Steven just stared at him. He laughed. "I'm going to tell Graeme." Alexander and Steven left Lucy enjoying the wildlife Internet sites and watched Graeme for a few moments.

"Can you set up instant messaging, Graeme, while Steven and I go back to Aunt Rhoda's house? Then we could chat on line. I'll show Steve."

"Yep! No problem!" Graeme grinned.

Mum drove them back to the site, promising to collect Lucy later. Alexander took Steven upstairs to his laptop. "Sometimes we chat to my dad on line," he explained, "But ordinary e-mail's cheaper." He switched on. "It's battery-operated, and it has a mobile phone line. Otherwise we'd be running up Aunt Rhoda's phone bill all the time." He was clicking as he spoke.

"This is me: Bulls Fan AC." He pulled his sweater off to reveal the red basketball vest he was wearing underneath. "I support the Chicago Bulls, see. And my password is just 'BullsAC'." He typed it in, and Steven saw the asterisks appear.

At the top of the screen there was a window with a list of four names. He didn't know two of them, but one was Jonathan Curtis, and the last was Graeme. He called himself ProfGR.

"Look, the little person next to his name is flashing green," Alexander explained. "That means he's on line and waiting."

Hi. How many people at the cafe? Alexander typed.
About 25. Graeme replied.
How long R U staying? Alexander wrote back.
All day. Graeme wrote back.

Steven was intrigued. "But if you really wanted to say something, wouldn't it be easier to phone?"

"I guess so. But on line, you can have a three-way conversation, and anyway, it's much more fun!"

Three days to go to the parade. Steven sent an instant message on Wednesday to Graeme, on duty as usual at the Internet café: How many people?
At least 40. Graeme wrote back.

The numbers increased all week, and the day before the parade, Graeme announced that he was going to stay in the café because he didn't want it to have to close while the procession drove round the neighbourhood. Steven agreed to stay with him once he had waved off the procession.

Chapter 11

The parade

"The sun has got his hat on, hip hip hip hooray!" Lucy sang as she ran down the stairs two at a time on Saturday morning. "Hurry up everybody! It's Parade Day!" she called.

Steven chuckled. He himself had been awake and dressed for ages. He was already downstairs eating breakfast. He watched her tear the final sheet from the green block, and throw it in the bin.

"Lucy! It's only six o'clock!" came Dad's sleepy, grumpy voice from under the bedclothes. But it wasn't long before he appeared, yawning and groping for the kettle. "Anyone would think it was Christmas," he muttered.

"Better put your Santa suit on then, Dad!" Steven grinned. Dad grunted, made tea and toast, and took a tray upstairs for himself and Mum.

It was almost an hour later when Steven called up the stairs, "Come on, Mum, Dad." He couldn't sit still any longer. Lucy was doing twirls around the kitchen in her paint-spattered artist's smock, and waving a paintbrush.

There was some shuffling in the hall, then Mum's voice boomed, "Ho! You down there! Small fry! Bring out your champion!"

"Come in, Mum! Let's see!" Lucy squeaked.

Slowly, the kitchen door opened, and Goliath appeared in the kitchen. Mum was wearing a wig of long, unkempt black hair, and a huge beard. She had enormous boots, which made her several centimetres taller than usual. Over her black leggings and a black T-shirt, her armour was shimmering silver. She carried a big plastic sword and shield. Steven and Lucy cheered and clapped. Mum grinned through her beard, and said, "You haven't seen anything yet! Just wait!"

She walked stiffly to the table and sat down with difficulty, not wanting to crease the foil. All eyes were focused on the doorway. "Come on, Dad!" Lucy called, jumping up and down. Suddenly the hall was filled with a cacophony of sound: jangling, piping and crashing.

Steven stared in disbelief. Dad was completely unrecognisable. He pranced into the kitchen – a one-man-band, wearing a harlequin clown suit and playing a tin whistle. His costume was all in one, made of shiny satin, cut in multi-coloured diamond shapes. Little bells hung from the sleeves, cuffs and ankles, and jangled as he danced. He had cymbals strapped to the insides of his knees, and he clashed them as he jigged up and down. His wig was a mop of yellow wool, and his face...! Steven gasped. He was a clown with white base make-up, a red lipstick mouth and black crinkly marks round his eyes. Steven began to laugh. This was a new Dad. One he had never met before. And he felt proud of him! Proud that he wasn't afraid to make a fool of himself and join in wholeheartedly. And what a brilliant fool!

Lucy got up to hug him. "Don't touch!" Dad

warned, laughing. "You'll smudge my make-up!"

"Dad, you're fantastic!" Steven told him.

"Well, son, I thought that if you could deliver a speech from a JCB shovel with everyone staring at you, I could cope with dressing up for the Holiday Club float."

"However did you get the idea?" Lucy persisted.

"I thought, I mustn't let Amanda down. I've got to be a good advert for the Holiday Club. It's got to be colourful, noisy, active, with never a dull moment!"

"Just like the Holiday Club!" Lucy said approvingly.

"But where did you get the suit?" Steven went on.

"Oh, I confess I hired it. From a fancy-dress shop in Glasgow."

"And what about the make-up?" Steven persisted.

"That was my handiwork," Mum said proudly. "I got a book from the library about face-painting."

"Trouble is," Dad said mournfully, "Mum's told me I'm not allowed to eat anything all day, because I'll spoil my lipstick!"

With lots of giggling and last minute grabbing of necessary equipment, the four of them got into the van. First they drove out to the MacKay farm where they all transferred to the float, which had been parked in a barn overnight. Then they drove into the village where Mr and Mrs MacKenzie and Amanda were standing together in the square, putting last minute finishing touches to the children's sheep costumes. Mr Johnstone's grandson, Chris, dressed as David the shepherd boy, stood still and tall, grasping his shepherd's crook firmly. Everyone climbed on board, and took up their positions for a practice.

Steven soon spotted Alexander and Graeme wandering around, admiring the costumes and decorations. "Where's your mum, Alexander? And Mrs Granny?" he asked them.

"They had things to finish off," Alexander replied. "They're coming in a few minutes."

"Hello, lads! How're you doing?" It was Mr Fergusson with his police dog, Prince.

"Fine, thanks, Mr Fergusson. Is Prince going on the float with you?"

"Aye, Steven. He's never been one to miss a bit of excitement, our Prince. He knows when he's on to a good thing."

"Which is your float?" Alexander asked, looking round.

"Sandy Campbell's gone to get it. He's picking the six of us up at the end of the street in half an hour. Prince and I thought we'd come and see what's going on."

The four of them looked up and down the High Street and Prince sniffed the breeze. There was bunting fluttering from the shop fronts, and every lamp post had a hanging flower basket. The village was humming with music and happy, noisy activity.

"The Internet café has been a great success, lads. Well done!" Mr Fergusson said. "How much longer has it got to run?"

"Just one more week," Graeme replied. It's going to finish on Friday because it's the marathon and prize giving on Saturday.

"I should think it's in line for a prize."

"Not really," Graeme said, with just a hint of regret. "People have enjoyed it, but it hasn't made all that much money."

"Well, I'd say it's been a roaring success. And there's more ways than just money to measure success!" Mr Fergusson declared. "Must get going, lads. Enjoy yourselves."

"I'm off to see how the café's going," Graeme announced. "I'll be back at ten o'clock to watch the procession set off." He made his way through the colourful crowds towards the high school, out of sight.

"Where are they?" Alexander said, looking around anxiously for his mum and Mrs Granny. "I want them to see the Holiday Club float, and your dad in the driving seat. They're going to miss the fun! I think we should go round and tell them to hurry up. Anyway, I just don't know what's holding them up."

"By the time we get there and back we'll miss the fun, as well," Steven objected.

"Not if we borrow a couple of bikes. We can be there in five minutes if we go now. The newsagents is only across the square. Mr and Mrs Mitchell have got bikes. I guess they'd lend them if we promise to be careful."

"OK," Steven sighed, and turned to look properly at Alexander. His face was white. Steven suddenly realised that Mrs Curtis wasn't the only one who worried about the casino men.

As they rode like the wind back to the caravan site they met lots of people walking towards the village, and lots more already lining the road where the procession was due to pass by. "If everyone standing here puts some money in the collecting tins, we'll make a fortune!" Steven panted.

They rode in at the gate of the cottage. The caravan site was deserted. In the lane outside the site, a big shiny car was parked. "I don't recognise that," said Steven. "Looks like someone's got rich visitors."

They dumped the bikes outside Mrs Granny's garden, and Steven paused, suddenly wary. But Alexander dashed in at the back door, calling "Hi! Mom? Aunt Rhoda?" There couldn't have been anyone in the kitchen, because Steven saw Alexander go through the kitchen into the hall, leaving the back door open.

Following on behind, Steven stopped. Something was not quite right. He held his breath and listened. Voices were coming from the sitting room. Men's voices.

"Ah! Here's our young friend! Chip off the old block, he is! Just like his father!"

"You on your own, then, young man? What're you doing here?"

"Er, I just came to see why Mom was late!" Alexander replied in a voice that sounded higher than usual.

"Let go of him! He's just a boy. He's not going to do you any harm!" It was Mrs Granny, but her voice didn't sound quite normal, either. Steven let his breath out slowly and shrank into the dining room doorway. From there, he could see through the narrow crack where the sitting room door stood ajar. A man in a dark suit was standing with his back to the fireplace. Steven had never seen him before. He could see Mrs Curtis, sitting on the sofa, her back to the door. He couldn't see Mrs Granny or Alexander. Neither could he see the second man who began to speak.

"We're not here to bother you, ladies." His words were kind, but his voice was harsh, and Steven was immediately on his guard. His heart began to hammer so hard he thought it might give him away. "But we need to know your husband's whereabouts. We need to be able to contact him by phone right now."

"But I tell you, I don't know where he is." It was Mrs Curtis's voice. "He went back to the States to sort out our affairs."

"Leaving a lovely wife and smart son here in the backwoods of Scotland? I don't think so," said the man at the fireplace. "I need you to get him on this phone right now, lady, or that pretty face might be marred for ever!" He pulled a packet of cigarettes and a lighter from his pocket. Lighting up, he took a long draw on the cigarette. Steven could see the end glowing red. Then the man took a step towards Mrs Curtis, and began to wave it in her face. Terror squeezed its icy fingers around Steven's heart. Something heavy seemed to be lodging in his throat. Mrs Curtis moaned and moved from side to side, away from the threat of being burned.

"No!" Alexander shouted, lunging towards the man with the cigarette. Steven gasped. Now he could see Alexander's back, and he could see the arms of the second man, who grabbed him and pinned an arm roughly behind his back. Alexander whimpered for a moment.

Steven looked round wildly. If he went out again, through the back door, the man at the fireplace would surely see him. Mrs Granny never used the front door. She kept the key on a hook in the hall. Steven knew he couldn't unlock it and get out silently. The phone was on the wall beside the kitchen, but by the time he had dialled 999 the men would be on to him, and their threats were clearly no joke. But he had to do something quickly.

As he tried to think, he heard them talking about Mr Curtis' gambling debts, and how he was a dishonest man who didn't pay his dues. Steven looked upstairs. It was the only place he could get to without being seen from the sitting room door.

"We don't like people who don't pay up!" the man holding Alexander was saying. His voice was low, gravelly and mean.

Steven crept towards the stairs. Exasperated, he knew Mrs Granny didn't have a phone upstairs. Mum had tried to nag her into getting one fitted when she was so ill before Easter, in case she needed help in the night. But she had never got around to it. So he couldn't phone. He'd have to climb out of a window, and down to the ground. He'd have to run to the cottage and phone from there.

"She's telling the truth!" Mrs Granny was objecting, her voice a bit wobbly. "The only way we can contact him is by e-mail."

E-mail! That was it! Instant messaging! Steven reached the top of the stairs and stopped for a moment to listen. They were still talking. He could hear Mrs Granny pleading, trying to reason with the men. No one had heard him.

Tiptoeing into Alexander's room, he saw the laptop on a small table near the window. If only, he thought. If only he could remember how to go on line and contact Graeme directly. If only Graeme could be sitting at the computer right now. He took a deep breath and let it out slowly. Please Lord, he prayed silently. Please help me now. He opened up the laptop and switched it on. Come on, he pleaded silently. Come on. What to do first? He'd never used it without Alexander. He searched the screen, trying to remember. There it was. The instant messager icon. He clicked, then typed in Alexander's password: BullsAC. Then he looked at the list. Graeme's person was flashing green. Yes! With his fingers trembling and feeling like thumbs, he began to type:

need help.

mrs granny and mrs c and A in truble

get police to come to mrs grannys house quick.
Steven

He pressed 'send', then he clenched his fists and waited. Sure enough, Graeme was there! Thank you, Lord, he breathed.

Graeme wrote: What's happening? Why do you need the police?

Steven nearly yelled with frustration. How could Graeme start a conversation just now when any second Mrs Curtis or Mrs Granny might get hurt? He wrote again.

no time to xplain

danger

get help

This time there was no reply, so he had to assume Graeme had gone for help. He looked at his watch. Ten thirty. The procession must have begun their slow drive through the village. Lucy would be painting pictures on the Holiday Club float. Mum would be doing her bit, acting Goliath. Dad would be driving, with everyone staring at him in amazement. The whole village would be busy. No one would miss Steven or Alexander. Everyone would assume they were helping with the Internet café. Graeme was his only hope.

Steven tiptoed to the window, hoping desperately that the floorboards wouldn't squeak. He was looking for a drainpipe, or anything to help him climb out. But there was nothing. Just a sheer drop on to a concrete path.

Still the voices droned on downstairs. The men were trying to wear Mrs Curtis down, to force her to give up Mr Curtis' hiding place. Steven wished he could be contacted, then the men might go and leave them alone.

Straining his ears to hear exactly what they were saying, Steven heard a different sound. Not the nee-naw of an emergency vehicle as he had hoped, but a distant racket, getting nearer and growing louder all the time. There were horns sounding, trumpets playing, cymbals, drums, shouting and singing.

Peering up the lane, Steven saw the procession with its flags waving jauntily in the breeze, its colourful actors laughing and waving and all its happy, noisy activity approaching Mrs Granny's house. He gasped with delight and relief, wondering only for a moment about the fact that this was not on the procession's planned route.

Leading the procession was the police float, with recruitment posters stuck all around it, and half a dozen smart, uniformed men waving. Prince sat alert among them. Sandy Campbell was driving. Steven looked again. Graeme was up front, sitting beside him!

Following the police float was the flower-arranging club. They were using a milk float beautifully decorated with flowers from top to bottom. The women sitting in it and the driver wore flowers, too.

Now, Steven could see the Holiday Club float, fourth or fifth in line. There was Dad, a bright figure in the driver's seat. Mum was swishing her sword from side to side. And there was Chris, Lucy, Amanda and the little kids in sheep costumes.

He could see them all, and he began to wave and beckon frantically, but no one was looking in his direction. Even if he shouted, no one would hear him above all the racket.

Then to Steven's joy and amazement, he saw Sandy Campbell indicate to the driver behind, and he pulled the police float off the road to stop on the grass verge. The rest of the floats veered around it and continued on their noisy, cheerful journey. Steven saw Sandy Campbell, Ronnie Fergusson and five other men leap from the float and run towards Mrs Granny's back door. Steven dashed downstairs, just in time to see the two dark-suited men run straight into their arms!

"Morning, Steven!" Sandy Campbell said cheerfully. "Enough excitement for you?"

Chapter 12

Fitting the pieces together

An hour later, after police cars from the police station in the Old Town had come to take the two men away, Sandy Campbell gave the three boys, Mrs Granny and Mrs Curtis a lift to the Internet café, then drove the police float back to rejoin the procession.

"Come and have a cup of coffee, Mom," Alexander urged, taking his mother protectively by the arm, as they went into the café together and placed their order.

"So why didn't you phone 999?" Steven asked Graeme, sinking his teeth into a doughnut.

"I thought you might be joking," Graeme replied. "I didn't want to be arrested for wasting police time or something!"

"Joking!" Steven spluttered, almost choking on his doughnut. Even in the safety of the Internet café, with familiar faces all around him, his insides still went cold with horror at the thought of the cigarette waving in front of Mrs Curtis' face. "Would I really joke about something like that?"

"Well, I kept thinking about the haunted forest, last Easter, and Alexander and the ghost wolves..."

"OK, OK," Steven admitted.

"So," Graeme continued, "the next best thing I could think of was to tell Sandy Campbell. So I ran to the village square and they were all just setting off. You should have heard the racket! And your dad, Steven..."

"What did he do?" Alexander demanded.

"Wait 'till everyone comes back," Steven said, "Then you'll see him."

"Anyway," Graeme went on, "Sandy said he didn't think you would joke at a time like this. So he told me to hop in, and said he'd lead the procession on a detour past Mrs Granny's house, and check it out."

"I sure am glad he did!" Alexander said. "Hey, Graeme! Here's your mom!"

"Hello, Mum!" Graeme said cheerfully. "Where've you been?"

"I watched the parade set off, then I went for a run along the beach and back up to the caravan park for a shower. Have you been here all the time?"

The three boys roared with laughter, leaving Mrs Curtis and Mrs Granny to explain.

It was mid-afternoon by the time Steven's dad had driven them all on Farmer MacKay's trailer back to Mrs Granny's house with takeaway pizzas from the village. They sat outside in the sun, Lucy and Mum still in their costumes. Dad insisted on getting changed and cleaned up, though there were still traces of make-up on his face.

While Steven went inside to help Mrs Granny dish up ice cream for dessert, Mrs Curtis went upstairs to check her e-mail. As they carried the bowls outside, they all heard her exclaim.

"Run upstairs, dear, and see if your mum's all right," Mrs Granny told Alexander.

After a few minutes, the two of them reappeared. Mrs Curtis was smiling, but tearful.

"Oh, Anne-Marie, what a day you've had," said Mum sympathetically, and went to put an arm round Mrs Curtis.

"Yes, it has been quite a day," Mrs Curtis agreed, sniffing and grinning, "but it has gotten better and better!"

"What do you mean?" Dad asked, putting his spoon down.

"Well, Alan, I had an e-mail from Jonathan." She gulped and swallowed. "And he said he was sorry. He apologised for messing everything up for us as a family. He said he still wasn't sure he'd been able to sort things out with Will, but there is a possible solution. And..." Another tear trickled down her cheek, even though she was smiling. "And, he said he was sorry he'd tried to push ahead with developing Hooper's Reach. He said that you, Steven, had been a very brave young man, and he admires you!"

"But you shouldn't be crying if it's good news, Mrs Curtis," said Lucy, frowning.

"I know, honey," said Mrs Curtis, getting up to give Lucy a quick hug. "I'm crying because I'm so happy. It's the first time he has said that he agrees with me. With us," she corrected herself, smiling at Alexander. "And the first time he has said he misses us!"

"So, do you think he'll come back if he manages to sort things out with Uncle Will, Mom?" Alexander asked.

"Who knows, honey. There's all that stuff with the casino to sort out, too."

"Do you know what I think, Mrs Curtis?" Lucy asked, pulling her garden chair up closer.

"What's that, honey?"

"I think you should eat your ice cream before it melts!"

Chapter 13
Marathon and prize giving

"Only three more days to go," Lucy remarked sadly, tearing a piece of paper from the last block. "Whatever will we do after the marathon and the prize giving?"

Mum and Dad laughed. "You're not usually short of ideas, love," Mum said.

"We'll help to rebuild the old lifeboat station, of course!" Steven exclaimed.

There was a tap on the back door, and Graeme put his head round. "Hi! My dad's here. We're going down to the beach so my mum can do some running. Want to come?"

"Yes, please!" Steven and Lucy chorused. So, while they went upstairs to fetch their things, Graeme's mum and dad stepped into the kitchen for a chat.

"Came to watch my better half win the marathon!" Steven heard Mr Robertson say.

"Win!" Mrs Robertson exploded. "I'll be lucky to finish!"

Steven grabbed his swimming shorts, a towel and a ball and ran downstairs again. "So it's all been sorted out?" Mr Robertson was saying.

"Almost. But there's still the matter of—"

"Hey, guys!" Alexander burst in at the back door, his eyes shining, his face red with excitement.

"What?" Lucy demanded, reappearing from upstairs.

"Sandy Campbell's just been round. Those men from the casino were frauds! Swindlers! Their gambling joint was twisted! Dad was right. They've been arrested and charged for dishonest practice, not just for threatening my mom!" He flopped on to a chair, out of breath.

"Wow! That's great news, Alexander," Dad said, clapping him on the back. "Bet your mum's pleased."

"She's on cloud nine!" Alexander agreed. "Oh, er, hi Mr Robertson, Mrs Robertson. Sorry, I didn't mean to..."

"That's all right, son," Mr Robertson smiled. "Glad to hear your good news after all that's happened. We were just going down to the beach. Do you want to come? Good job we've got a big car..."

Steven went with Alexander to fetch his things. At the back of Steven's mind was a vague memory of something Mrs Curtis had said. He tried to drag it to the front. "Hang on. Didn't your mum say that your dad thought they were cheats? When he was sober, in the morning, he could remember the details clearly, and he said the organisation wasn't run properly?"

"Yeah," Alexander agreed thoughtfully. "He doesn't owe anyone any money, and we've just e-mailed him to tell him. He even said there's a chance that everything's getting sorted out with Uncle Will, too."

"D'you think he might come back here, then?" Steven asked.

"I don't know. I sure hope so."

They walked in silence for a moment, then Alexander asked, "Remember the skipping rope?"

"What?"

"The skipping rope. Mr MacKenzie put it back together."

"Oh! Yeah!" Steven was suddenly all ears.

"Well, I was just hoping..."

Steven could tell Alexander was struggling.

"...Hoping that God would put it back together for your family?"

"Yeah. You know, Mrs Granny's hoping Dad will come back and stay with us all again. I thought she'd never want to see us again. Especially Dad."

"She's never stopped praying for you all," Steven told him.

"She's so brave! She was really cool when those men were in the house."

"It's because she knows she'll go to heaven," Steven said. "It was the same when she was ill. She wasn't scared because she knows she belongs to God, so she'll go to heaven."

Alexander didn't say anything, and they walked to Mrs Granny's house thoughtfully.

The last week of the school holiday slid away quietly compared with the previous weeks. The Internet café closed, with much regret from the villagers, old and young, who had enjoyed it. But the last few fund-raising events still drew enthusiastic crowds.

On Saturday, the Curtises, the Robertsons and Mrs Granny accompanied Steven and his family to the field beside the beach where the half marathon was to end, to cheer for Mrs Robertson and watch the exhausted competitors arrive.

"How many people entered?" Mrs Curtis asked Graeme.

"I think Mum said there were ninety-eight. But they might not all finish," Graeme replied.

"D'you think your mom will finish?" Alexander asked.

"She said she was determined to finish, but she said we might have to stay here a long time to see her!" Graeme said, grinning.

"What time will they get here?" Lucy asked, hopping impatiently from foot to foot.

"They reckon the first few people will arrive at about four o'clock, but goodness knows how long the stragglers will take," Mr Robertson told her.

Steven glanced at his watch. Three forty-five. He looked up and down the field that sloped away to the beach. Dozens of people had turned out to cheer the runners. They lined the ropes that had been rigged up to cordon off the spectators and give the runners space to reach the finishing ribbon.

Suddenly, a cry went up: "Here they come!" Everyone surged up to the ropes, craning their necks and straining their eyes to see who was winning.

"It's Ronnie Fergusson!" Dad shouted, and everyone began to clap and cheer as the burly policeman ran along the field, his face as red as his Aberdeen strip, and sweat pouring down his neck.

Steven and Lucy jumped up and down to get a better view. One of the PE teachers from the high school came next, then a group of people Steven didn't know. There was a short gap, then Sandy

Campbell puffed past, with his wife running beside him.

"How could she run all that way in a dress and sandals!" Lucy exclaimed. "She's not even out of breath!"

"She hasn't run all that way," Mum chuckled. "She's just joined Sandy at the bottom of the field to give him moral support!"

Graeme and his dad were silent, leaning on the rope, staring without blinking towards the remaining runners. "Here she comes!" Graeme shouted suddenly. "And who's that, running with her?"

At the bottom of the field, a tall fair-haired man wearing beige trousers, a short-sleeved red shirt and loafers had joined her, and was running alongside.

"Oh!" Alexander gasped. "It's my dad!" And he ducked under the rope, yelling "Dad! Dad!" and ran right into his dad's arms, with his mum close behind.

Graeme followed under the rope, and ran to complete the last hundred metres with his mum, cheering and clapping with the crowds. Beyond the finishing ribbon groups of exhausted, sweating runners were walking round trying to get their breath back, or lying flat out on the grass, their chests heaving. Mrs Robertson gave her number in at the judges' table and joined the MacGregors. The Curtises arrived at the same time, their arms around each other.

Official helpers in green tracksuits wandered among the milling crowds of runners, supporters and spectators, selling orange squash in paper cups for twenty pence. Mr Robertson bought a trayful, handing over five pounds and waving away the change. "It should be champagne!" he said, holding his cup high. "Here's to successful finishers—"

"—And returned wanderers!" Mrs Granny finished for him. "Welcome home, Jonathan!"

Mr Curtis smiled and drank the juice. "It sure is good to be back," he said. "They told me at the caravan site that there was an event down at the beach, so I came looking for a familiar face, and I found one." He grinned at Mrs Robertson. "A little redder than usual, but then, so is mine."

"It OK, Jonathan," Steven's mum assured him. "You've no need to feel embarrassed. It's all in the past."

"Mum! You came twentieth!" Graeme announced, running up from the judges' table.

"Congratulations, love," said Mr Robertson, giving her a kiss on the cheek.

"Come on, everyone," Steven urged them. "We mustn't be late for the award ceremony!"

"I think you should run in the next half-marathon, Steve," Dad grinned. "It might use up some of your surplus energy."

After the runners had had time to shower and change, the prize giving took place in the village hall. The place was too packed for them all to find seats together, so they piled in wherever they could. Graeme and Steven leaned against a side wall near the front of the hall. Everyone wanted to know who had won the fund-raising competition, but even more important, whether enough money had been raised or promised to enable the plans to go ahead to rebuild the old lifeboat station.

Finally, Mr MacKenzie, the spokesman for the

evening, called for quiet and began a long list of the monies raised by various organisations and efforts with much encouraging praise for everyone's hard work. Just when Steven was deciding it was boring, and he'd rather go home after all, Mr MacKenzie reached the interesting part.

"Now, ladies and gentlemen, the bit you've all been waiting for – the competition winners. The village council originally agreed that the winner would be the person whose idea raised the most money for the project, but it has been universally acknowledged that money is not always the most important consideration."

Come on, thought Steven. Come on.

"In a village like ours," Mr MacKenzie continued, community life is just as important, indeed, in many cases more important than money." There were some murmurs of agreement from the crowd, and Mr MacKenzie smiled as he went on. "So we have decided to award two prizes of equal status. One of these goes to Sergeant Sandy Campbell. Last week's parade was his idea, and thanks to the generosity of the townspeople and the residents of all the neighbouring villages, the money raised has exceeded all our expectations."

Wild cheering and clapping accompanied this announcement, and Sandy went forward to receive his prize and a handshake. Mr MacKenzie added thanks from the whole village for all the work that Sandy had put in as co-ordinator.

"But the other first prize," Mr MacKenzie was continuing, "goes to two lads without whose creative ideas this whole project would never have got underway."

Graeme dug Steven in the ribs. Steven's heart was beginning to thud with a mixture of hope and nerves.

"Two lads who make an excellent team because they combine a mixture of know-how and enthusiasm. Ladies and gentlemen, please give a big hand for Steven MacGregor and Graeme Robertson!" He beckoned them up on to the stage, and as they wove their way through the crowds, Steven looked down the hall. There were hundreds of people there. The back doors of the hall were open, and people who couldn't find a place inside were crowding round, trying to see in. Among them, Steven recognised Colin Henderson.

"The Internet café has become a focal point of our village over the past two weeks," Mr MacKenzie told the crowd once the clapping had died down. "Countless people have told me how they've always wanted a gentle beginning to computing, and with the help of Mr Jimmy Johnstone and his colleagues from the high school computing department, not to mention our young friend here," he clapped Graeme on the shoulder, "they've had exactly that. Youngsters have been able to get together there on rainy evenings, and the café has really put the village on the map and brought us into the twenty-first century. Well done lads!" He shook their hands and presented them with envelopes. Steven could hardly wait to look inside.

After more cheers, Mr MacKenzie said, "Lads, have you got anything to add? Graeme, it was your brainwave, wasn't it?"

"Well, yes," said Graeme, standing awkwardly at the front of the stage, "but it was Steven who persuaded me that the idea might work."

"Well done, Steven," Mr MacKenzie said again. "Any comments? Any more brainwaves to put into practice?"

"Um, just one," Steven admitted, clenching his fists to screw up his courage. "It would be great to have a permanent community Internet café at the old lifeboat station once it's turned into a visitors' centre!"

There was a moment's silence as everyone tried to take in this news. Then a swell of enthusiastic murmurs filled the hall.

"Wow!" said Graeme softly, right next to him.

"Actually," Steven said urgently to Mr MacKenzie, "it wasn't our idea. It was Colin Henderson's."

"Colin Henderson, eh?" said Mr MacKenzie, clearly trying to hide his surprise. "In that case, well done, Colin!"

Steven searched for a glimpse of Colin amongst the faces at the back door of the hall. He found him, and Colin gave Steven a thumbs-up sign before turning and leaving the crowd.

"That's quite some idea," Mr MacKenzie was saying. "We'd need someone with some expertise, time and hard cash to get that one up and running! But we'll see what we can do! What do you think?" He turned to the audience.

"Yes! Go for it!" someone shouted. The whole room broke into enthusiastic clapping and cheering, and it was a minute or two before Mr MacKenzie could make himself heard.

When it was finally quiet enough, he said, "And in case anyone has forgotten what this whole project was about anyway, I'm proud to announce that if we can find architects, builders, carpenters and joiners, the rebuilding of the old lifeboat station will go ahead as soon as possible!" At this news, people jumped up and down and the whole room erupted in shouts of joy. Everyone congratulated each other, and with much backslapping and waving, the meeting came to an unofficial close.

"Carpenters and joiners!" Steven whispered to Graeme. "That's what Colin Henderson wants to do, and he needs a job!"

Steven and Graeme stepped down from the platform, and in a corner beside the steps, they opened their envelopes. "Wow!" Steven breathed. "Discount Warehouse vouchers!" The amount was bigger than anything he had dared to hope for. "I can get tools, or bicycle parts or anything!"

"Or software!" Graeme added, equally delighted.

As everyone was filing slowly out of the hall, Steven was suddenly struck by such an enormous idea that he stood stock-still. It was one of those ideas that felt like God was working things out.

"Come on, slowcoach, I want to get back. I'm starving. Mr Curtis said he was going to get some pizza," Graeme complained.

"I've had an idea!" Steven announced.

"Not another one!" Graeme teased him.

"No, listen. I'm serious," Steven pleaded. "Mr Curtis is back. He needs a job. The visitors' centre needs a manager, and if we can have an Internet café there it'll need to be a manager with computer skills and a lot of business know-how. Mr MacKenzie said so." Steven turned to look earnestly at Graeme. "Maybe Mr Curtis is the man for the job. It'd be so exciting if it worked. What do you think?"

"Sounds like that might be God's way of mending broken lives," Graeme suggested, looking straight at Steven.

Steven stared. He couldn't believe what he was hearing. "Do you, er, I mean, what…"

"Remember Mr MacKenzie's skipping rope trick? He said that God mends broken lives."

"Yes," Steven hesitated. "But are you…?"

"Yes," Graeme said, going a bit red. "I'm a Christian."

"But how, I mean, when…"

"It was you, and Lucy. You said you wanted to please God. And then there was Mrs Granny. She was so willing to invite Mr Curtis back, despite everything that happened last time. And when I think what I said when you gave your sandals away…" He looked down for a moment, embarrassed. "Then Mr MacKenzie said God could mend broken lives, and it looks like that's what's happening with the Curtises and Colin Henderson. God's love never runs out, even for scumbags like them. And me! So I prayed, and asked God to take me on."

"Yes!" Steven punched the air. It was a great end to a great holiday. "Let's pray that God will take the Curtises on, too," he told Graeme. "Only don't tell Mr Curtis anything about running the new visitors' centre yet."

"Why not?"

"He might forget to get the pizza. Come on, I'm starving."